RODEO RANCH

Center Point
Large Print

Also by Max Brand® and available from
Center Point Large Print:

Gunfighters in Hell
The Double Rider
Sunset Wins
Jigger Bunts
Stagecoach
The Wolf and the Man
Out of the Wilderness
Magic Gun
The Tracker
The White Streak

RODEO RANCH

A Western Duo

MAX BRAND®

CENTER POINT LARGE PRINT
THORNDIKE, MAINE

THE VALLEY OF JEWELS

I

It was so hot that nobody in Cherryville had the ambition to stand up and look to see what caused the dust cloud that was rolling toward us down the road. When that dust cloud dragged closer, we could see the nodding heads of a pair of mules, in the lead team, and, pretty soon, somebody said that it must be Buck Logan's mules.

That was right. It was Buck, and he brought the queerest load from the railroad that we had ever dreamed about. A load of lumber!

He pulled up at the watering trough, slipped the checks of his eight mules, and let them have a drink. And while they were drinking, the steaming smell of melting pitch came rolling from the heaped and shining lumber on that big wagon and stung our nostrils.

"Buck," said someone, "who might the lucky party be that's to get that lumber?"

Buck looked up and shifted his quid, but, when the lump was settled in his other cheek, he changed his mind about answering and started checking up his mules again, pulling their heads hard to get them away from the water. Even a mule, which is too mean to be hurt by hardly anything, is a lot better off without too much cold water after a long pull. Then Logan climbed up to his seat and called to his team, but, when they hit the collars, a mule in the swing span came back as if from a sore shoulder—and the load wasn't started.

We forgot about our question. We were all too busy calling advice and laughing at Buck and enjoying the show.

Buck got into a towering rage. He was right proud of that mule team. They had cost him a good deal of money and care. He'd been here and he'd been there, getting sizes and colors that matched, and now he had a perfect set. They were all of the same gray shade to a hair. They tapered from big, sixteen-hand wheelers to mean, jack-rabbity-looking leaders, faster and smarter than you would believe. That team could pull a mountain of lead.

However, the watering trough had been overflowing, and the ground was streaked with mud, into which one of the fore wheels had worked down. So Buck had a time giving his team a hitch to the left and then a hitch to the right, and trying to break that wheel out of the mud and get the wagon rolling.

It was a big load, and a couple of those mules were sore-shouldered. Even the best care in the world couldn't keep a mule or a horse from having its shoulders knocked up if they worked those rough mountain roads.

By this time nobody had any foolish idea that

Buck would waste time answering questions about where that load of fine lumber was going. He was simply white with rage, to be shamed by his team in front of so many folks. And of course we made him feel it. A hardy fellow like Buck, with a vanity about mules, couldn't be turned loose without feeling the whip. If he laid the lash on his team, we laid the lash on Buck. We even managed to stand up to do it.

Rod Gruger said: "It's a shame how a mule team will run downhill. That was a likely enough team about six months back. And now look at them . . . they can't pull a paperweight off of a greased skid."

He said this sympathetically, and, shaking his head, went on: "If Buck was a fellow who would take advice, it's about time that somebody should up and tell him that a mule team like that is worth good care and good food. You can't give 'em thistledown for fodder and expect them to get fat. What about it, boys?"

We agreed in a chorus, I can tell you. And Buck, he pretended not to hear, but all the time his neck kept getting redder and redder, and all the time he was getting a straighter set on his mouth. Every now and then he cursed us out of the corner of his mouth. He was a hardy-looking fellow, Buck Logan. I never seen a two-handed fighter that looked more of the part than Buck did.

But what nearly drove him mad now was the knowledge that there was nothing that human care could give to those mules that they didn't get from him. He never worked them too hard, and he was always slaving at their harness, or going out of his way to haul in supplies of crushed barley for them. And he could have made twice as much money out of them, if he had only been willing to treat them like mules and not like babies.

However, we had our good time with him.

I jumped down and got my roan horse, Jupe, and led him around in front of the big mule team. He was about as big as a minute, though he was the hardiest little jack rabbit that ever bucked off a saddle or followed a calf like a snake through a herd.

"Hey, Buck," I said, "just pass me out that extra fifth chain that you got under your wagon, and I'll pull you out with Jupe, here."

That was more than Buck could stand. He threw down his blacksnake, and he yanked the four-horse whip out of the socket and came for me.

I barely had enough time to climb into the saddle before the lash of that whip screamed past my ear. It would almost have cut off my head if it had hit me, but I got away, with a yell. Old Jupe nearly jumped out of his skin to get from the path of that whip.

Buck threw his hat down in the dust and

stamped on it, he was so mad, and the boys on the verandah nearly died. They simply hung onto one another and cried, they had to laugh so hard. But after a while Buck went around to his mules, and he said something at the head of each one of them and gave them a slap on the neck.

It was a wonderful thing to see him take them in hand. They had been getting more and more restless, listening to the yelling and the foolishness of that gang of cowpunchers on the porch, but Buck quieted them down, and then he went back and jumped up on the back of his near-wheeler and laid his hand on the jerkline.

You could fairly see every ear in that procession of mules tip back to listen to the voice of the boss. Buck yelled, and that near leader stepped forward and took up the slack in the fifth chain, and the rest of the mules leaned just enough into the collars to get the kinks out. Then the blacksnake cut the air and cracked, and Buck yelled again.

Well, it was a pretty sight. Some people can't see anything in horseflesh except the racers with their long pedigrees and their fancy ways, but I've always seen a good deal in a work horse. They're an honest lot, you know. And work mules come right next for my admiration.

Those eight mules leaned into their collars. They scratched like dogs until they worked the way through that surface dust and got down to a firm footing, but, when their little hoofs held, they just stiffened their legs and hung in the collars, with their hips sinking down, and the harness standing high up above their backs.

It did a man good to watch them. And that wagon lurched, staggered, and then got out of the rut—and there was the mule team breaking into a trot to keep the wagon from running over them.

We liked Buck in spite of the queer ways he had, and we couldn't help giving him a cheer when he got his heavy wagon out as slick as all that.

Meanwhile, a dozen of us slid onto our horses and followed down the road to see where in the town he was going to leave that lumber.

But Logan didn't stop. He went right on through Cherryville and pointed the heads of those horses for the big rough mountains, where there was never a sign of a town within a good hundred miles.

II

Some of us thought that Buck must be mad; some of the rest thought that there might have been a new purchase of land in the last few weeks, and that this lumber was meant for building a new house. When we asked the sheriff—and he knew everything of importance that happened in the country—he said that there had been no sale. So where could Buck Logan have gone with that wagon?

We wished afterward that we had followed him right on. But a whole week went by before he hove through Cherryville bound in the same direction, and with another load of lumber. It was about dusk of the day, however, and there was nothing for Buck but to put up at the hotel.

We buzzed all around his team and his wagon while he was putting it up, and we tried everything but questions, because we knew that Buck was one of the most silent men in the world. But nothing came out of what we could see. At supper Buck sat down in the corner seat at the table—I mean he sat in the chair that was always for me, which will be explained as I go along.

Anyway, when I came in and saw Buck seated in that chair, the boys all grinned at me, very broad and very expectant. They thought that I would tackle Buck and tell him to get out of that chair. But that wasn't my style. I've never liked fighting. And if trouble has sat down beside me more than once in my life, it hasn't been because I've invited it. I didn't like to be away from my usual place, but I thought that I could stand it for one night. So I took a chair as near the other corner as I could. By hitching my chair around to the side a good deal, I could keep my eye on the two doors that opened into the room, and there was only one window that bothered me. It opened behind my shoulder, and every minute it was like a gun pointed at my back.

However, I was willing to accept that misery even if it gave me indigestion. It was better for me than hunting for a fight with Buck Logan. And nobody could expect to get that big Logan out of a chair without a fight.

Nothing would have come out of this, if it hadn't been that the boys couldn't keep their mouths shut. They had to start talking. And about the first thing they whispered was loud enough to fetch down the table to my ears, and therefore I knew that it must have got to the ears of Logan, too.

Some fool among the boys said: "It'll happen after the supper is over. Doc Willis will rip into Logan then and tear him to bits."

I could have murdered the boy who whispered

14

that. I didn't dare to look down the table, and yet from the corner of my eye I could see Buck Logan lifting his head like a lion and glaring at me. Altogether, it was what I'd call a mean situation. I've known killings to start with a lot less. A whole lot less.

But that was not all that happened, and that was not all that was said. There was a buzz and a murmuring on all the time. Most of it was for the benefit of Buck.

I finished my meal as fast as I could and got out on the verandah and wedged myself against the wall. But still it was a long time before the little chills stopped wriggling up and down my back. I finished my first cigarette, and then a couple of the boys came out, and big Buck Logan was at their heels. He rambled straight up to me and he sang out for me and the world to hear: "Say, kid, I understand that you're gonna eat me. Eat me raw and swaller me right down. Lemme hear what you think about it?"

He was plumb offensive, I must say, but I knew that the boys had been working Buck up to this point. He was a big man and a mean man in a silent sort of a way—which is the meanest of all—but he was not the sort of a fellow to hunt trouble. He had enough of that with his mules. So I looked him over and swallowed the first half dozen answers that jumped up to the tip of my tongue.

15

I merely said: "Logan, I think the boys have been talking a lot of bunk to you. I don't want any trouble with you. Not a bit. Sit down and make yourself at home." I pointed to the chair beside me and smiled at him. Nothing could have been friendlier than that, though I admit that it may have given him a pretty good excuse for thinking the thought that I saw in his face.

He simply wrinkled up with contempt and with disgust, and he turned around on his heel and strode off toward the barn.

I sat there rubbing my cheek, because I felt exactly as though I had been hit in the face.

I heard one of the lads break out: "By the heavens, Doc is going to take it."

And somebody else said: "Logan looks pretty big to him."

That lifted me right out of my chair, but after an instant I made myself settle down again. They could say what they pleased. The day had been—and not so very long before—when a pair of speeches like this would have made me go gunning for the biggest man in the world, with my teeth set. But I had had a good deal of the foolishness knocked out of me, and my nerves were a long distance from being what they had once been.

I had been insulted. There was no doubt of that. When a man refuses to answer a decent question and turns on his heel and walks away, it's enough insult to satisfy anybody, I suppose. But at the same time I couldn't help wanting to dodge the trouble if it were possible.

You see, Buck Logan was a square fellow, from what I'd seen and heard of him. At least, I'd seen him handle a mule team in a pinch without any brutality, and that was more than I could say about any other muleskinner I can recall. No, I felt that Buck Logan was a good fellow and that it would pay me a lot to avoid the bad side of him. As for these other fellows, let them say what they wanted to about me. Words are not one-ounce bullets. Not by a lot they aren't.

I made myself another cigarette and lit it and snapped the match off into the darkness. I felt that I was as cool and as calm as could be, but I was wrong. I was all brittle and ready to break, and it only took a snap of the fingers to do it.

Matter of fact, I'm ashamed to tell what set me off. But a grizzly old cat that belonged in the hotel came sauntering down the porch, and I wanted to show how easy and careless I was by pretending not to notice the eyes that were on me and the smiles and the wonder and the contempt that was showing on their faces. But when I reached out my hand and talked soft to the cat, it arched its back and spat at me, and then it jumped off the verandah into the night.

That brought a roar of laughter. I don't know

why, but it sent a rush of red-hot blood spinning into my brain. I jumped up from my chair and walked over where the rest of the boys were.

"Are you laughing at me?" I asked.

That sobered them. But even when they were silent, I was still raging.

"I asked you if you were laughing at me, by any chance? Do I hear you answer?"

Then somebody lost in the shadows in the rear drawled: "You better ask Buck Logan about that."

I yelled: "Curse Buck Logan! Some of you go tell him that I say he's a rat, and that if he don't come here to me, I'll go and find him . . . and there ain't any hole deep enough for him to hide in."

Then I began to walk up and down that verandah, hotter than ever. But I wasn't so angry that I didn't notice two or three of the boys detach themselves and wander off toward the barn. So I knew that Logan would hear what I had said, and hear it with trimmings, too. And I knew that that was apt to make for a gunfight—the very thing that I had dodged safely for two whole years, and that I had vowed I would never go through with again. However, a man can't change his nature. I was raised too much around guns. And I had spent too many years in Mexico—a wild and bad place, believe me.

After a little time I heard footsteps coming, and

in the lead there was a long, heavy stride that I figured must be Buck Logan. Yes, here he came, right up the steps out of the night, and stood there under the gasoline lamp.

I said to myself that he was as good as a dead man, that minute. I was full of concentrated poison, and full of concentrated coldness, too. What happens in moments like that are a blur to some people—a blur to most honest men, I suppose—but not to me. When the devil takes me by the throat he multiplies me by ten, and I felt the strength of ten in me at that moment.

I saw Buck Logan as complete as though he were painted by my hand in oils. I saw his faded blue shirt, and the wrinkles in his overalls around the knees, and the hard knot of his bandanna around his neck, and the sun-stained felt hat on his head. I saw the low, handy fit of the Colt at his right hip, too, and I looked through his pale-blue eyes into his soul and thought that he was as brave and as stern a man as I had ever seen in my life—but that made no difference. I was set for a kill, and I looked on Logan as a man living but already more than half dead.

He looked me over, too. He was just as calm as me, but there was no fire in his eyes. His hands were his best weapons, and not his guns—I could tell that, I thought.

Then he said: "Willis, I hear that you've been saying hard things about me."

"I'll say them over again, if you want to hear them," I said.

"I don't want to hear them," said Logan. "If I do hear them, I'll have to fight you. And I'm not ready to start pushing the daisies."

III

Well, take the time and the place and the rest into consideration, and you'll have to admit that was a good deal of a speech for a man to make. But though those boys who stood around and watched were a hardy gang as ever stepped, not one of them smiled and not one of them made the mistake of thinking that Buck was taking water. I didn't make that mistake, either.

I sat down again in my chair. I said: "Buck, the trouble was that you made a mite of a mistake about me . . . but I never made any mistake about you. I don't want any trouble with you if I can avoid it. I feel plumb friendly to you, if you'll give me a chance to act that way."

"Friend," Buck Logan said, "is a word that I don't use more than once every ten years, but maybe I could make an exception this evening. We'll shake hands, if you say the word."

Yes, we did shake hands, and when those big bony fingers of his closed over mine, they made me feel as weak as a baby. He sat down and turned his big head toward the others.

"Scatter, kids," he said. "This here is a time for man talk, and you're too young to listen."

They didn't wait to be invited twice. They just

21

faded away here and there, and we were left alone.

"It was the little roan horse," Buck said after a time.

I nodded. "Here's the makings," I said. "Smoke up."

He shook his head and pulled out a black pipe. Then he whittled some shavings off of a black plug, and filled his bowl with that stuff. When he lit up, a cloud of smoke that would have killed mosquitoes filled the air. There was no doubt about Buck being a man-size man. One whiff of that pipe smoke of his was enough to settle the question. It made me fair dizzy.

"It was the roan," Buck said again.

"Sure," I said, and nodded again. "I understand."

About ten minutes later he added: "My mules is close to me, Willis."

"Sure," I said. "I understand."

And, about half an hour later he said: "Time for me to turn in. This here was a fine talk, Willis." And he went off to bed.

You can count the words that had gone to the making of that "fine talk." But I felt that I knew Buck, and he felt that he knew me.

I turned out at the first crack of day, because I've ridden the range so long that the sun doesn't let me sleep late. When I came down, there were the mules all strung out in front of the load of lumber, and Buck hitching them in their places. He must have got up an hour before the light began, because he had that whole team fed and harnessed and curried down as slick as a whistle.

I stepped out and gave him a hand till he warned me to stop.

"They know their boss," Logan said, "but with strangers, they think that they're tigers and that they can live on raw meat. Mind the heels of that gray devil on the off point."

I side-stepped just as the heels of the off-pointer whistled past my ear.

Buck Logan stepped back to his place and took hold on the jerkline. "Look here, Doc," he said, "what's your job?"

"I still got most of a month's wages to blow in," I said.

"How come?"

"Poker has been good to me."

"Poker," he said, and grinned. "And then what?"

"I got the best cutting horse on the range," I said. "I'll pick me up a job, when that money is blowed in."

"Fine," he said. "Riding range?"

"Riding herd, I suppose."

"How about man-size work, Doc?"

"I dunno what you mean."

"Real pay."

"What kind?"

"Fifty a week."

I whistled. "That's better than ten," I admitted.

"Does it sound to you?"

"Not a bit."

"Why not? Like poker better?"

"No, poker always licks me in the end."

"Well?"

"I'm not a fifty-dollar-a-week man, Buck. Fifty a month is more to my style."

"No chances, eh?"

"Buck," I said, "how old am I?"

"Thirty-two," he answered, quick as a wink.

"You miss me by seven years," I told him.

"You're not thirty-nine," he said.

"I'm not."

"The devil," Buck said. "Are you only a kid of twenty-five?"

"I'm twenty-five," I stated, "but I'm not a kid."

"You wear your gray hair right along with me," he said. "And you ain't got the fool look."

"I've had the foolishness shot out of me," I told him.

He nodded. "I had a pal fifteen years ago that was that way. Quietest man that ever lived, but he was like you, one of these here lion tamers."

"Go easy, partner," I said.

"I'm not kidding you," said Buck Logan. "If you've been shot up so much that seven years have leaked out with the blood . . . why, I'm not

fool enough to talk down to you. Only this job
I'd . . ."

"I ain't tempted," I said.

"Why not?"

"I hate fighting."

"I didn't say that."

"No, but I guess that. Fifty a week in these
days means one of two things . . . crooked work
or guns. Well, you're not a crook, Buck."

"Thanks," he said. "But fifty a week is fifty a
week."

"It depends on how long the weeks last."

"I know, but this job is different. It ain't
dangerous, but it may be. You better saddle your
horse and come along."

"I have swore off on being a fool," I said.

"Swear on again," Buck said, "because you're
too young to miss the fun."

"Buck," I said, "it's fine of you . . . but it won't
do. I'd like to be with you, but I won't go."

He only grinned. "I've planted the poison in
you," said Buck. "I'm taking the creek road, and
I'll expect you to catch up with me by noon. So
long till then, kid."

He hollered to his mules. They hit their collars
with a snap, and the big wagon with its shining
load of white lumber rolled on down the road.

I turned my back on it after I had watched it
out of sight, but when I walked back to the hotel,
I heard a rumbling of distant thunder and turned

25

around with a start. I could see nothing, but I knew that that was the big wagon crossing the bridge and turning onto the creek road.

Who the devil would want to cart good lumber like that up the creek road? I had thought that Buck was joking when he told me that, but now I knew for certain that he had meant what he said, and the mystery of the thing began to work on me like wine in the blood.

Well, I turned my shoulder on the temptation as firmly as I could, and I went about the morning calmly enough. After breakfast I sat in at a three-handed game, and about 10:00 a.m. I had $150 stacked upon the table in front of me. I was in the middle of the neatest winning streak that I had ever started. The cards were for me. There was plenty of coin in that party, and I felt that I could drift my way to a year's holiday by noon. But all at once I had to jump up from my chair and push all my winnings back into the game.

"Boys," I said, "there's your cash. I can't sit this game out, and I won't quit while you still want revenge. So long."

They stared at me as though they thought that I was a madman, but I ran on up to my room, jerked my things together, and hurried out to the barn.

In five minutes more I was running Jupe up the trail. We came to the old Creek bridge—looking so rickety that I wondered how it could ever have stood the weight of the big wagon and its heavy load—but there was the track of the wheels, down the middle of it, and the great steel tires had sunk half an inch deep into the rotten surface.

I put Jupe at a hard run across that bridge and fanned him over the next hill with my quirt. After that I settled back in the saddle and took things easy, because I knew that I had committed myself so far on this expedition that I would not turn back.

It was later than noon before I sighted the dust cloud, however, for that team of mules knew how to step out on the road, and they could do four miles an hour when they had a fair chance. At least, so big Buck claimed for them, and I believe that he was right. They were the outwalkingest mules I ever saw.

But once I had the dust in sight, I was soon up with them. Buck turned around and gave me one dusty grin. Then he trudged on beside the wagon, and I jogged along behind.

I wasn't exactly contented. I felt that there was danger and bad danger ahead of us, some place. But I still couldn't figure what that danger might be.

"Hello," Buck said suddenly. "Look at that buzzard, there, just out of rifle range. Queer how much sense them birds has, old-timer, eh? Know to ten yards just how far a rifle bullet will carry."

I looked up and spotted that buzzard. It was wheeling pretty low down, as buzzards fly.

"I dunno," I said. "Looks to me that a bullet would fan the feathers out of that piece of misery."

"Humph!" said Buck.

"Well," I said, "I'll show you, if you got any doubts."

I pulled my Winchester out of its sheath. It was a good gun. Any Winchester is a sweet rifle, but this was extra tight and handy, and it shot as straight as a ruled line—or straighter when you got to know its habits. I tipped up the barrel, studied the flight of the buzzard, and followed it for a couple of seconds.

"Hurry up," Buck urged. "It's climbing."

It was climbing, well enough. You couldn't see a beat of the wings, but all at once that buzzard began to whirl around in its circle three times as fast as it had gone before. It was climbing fast, in the mysterious way that buzzards know. They may be things of horror to look at close up, but they're certainly things of wonder on the wing. And this black bit of mystery was fairly sliding off up into the heart of the sky. It was a long shot, but I got a good bead, and a pretty fair sense of the drift of the bird. Then I pulled the trigger.

"You see!" Buck called. "Out of range!"

"If I didn't hit that bird, I'm a liar," I said.

And just then the buzzard stopped sailing along

and tumbled fast for the ground. It hit with a thump fifty yards away, but neither of us had any curiosity about taking a closer look at it.

Then I looked aside at Buck Logan, and I saw that he was trying to look calm, but that he was really swallowing a lot of exultation. His face had the look of a man who says: "I told you so."

Even if I had not smelled a rat long before, one glance at that expression of Logan's would have been enough to convince me that we were bound for a place where there would be a premium on straight shooting and quick thinking. He was very pleased that I had brought that buzzard down, and I could see that the old rascal had been merely trying me out without asking me to show what I could do.

IV

It was about a day after this, that we turned to the left and headed through the hills over a road where the wheels sank deep and where the wagon stalled every couple of miles and the mules had to fight and struggle to get it rolling again.

I watched the course that we were taking, and all at once I yelled at Buck: "We're heading for the creek! We're going right straight for Daggett Creek!"

"Son," he said, "you talk sense, but why for shouldn't we be heading for Daggett Creek?"

"Why for shouldn't we? Why for should we, would be a lot more reasonable question to ask, I should say. Who would want to haul lumber to Daggett Creek . . . unless they're going to start up with a dude ranch there?"

"Son," Buck said, "you can keep on guessing until the time comes . . . which I hope that it will come to you easy, and not in a hard lump."

That was all he would say. But there we were, aimed across the white hills of the desert plumb in the direction of the creek.

I said to Buck: "Tell me the truth. Some sucker thinks that he can strike gold there again."

"Maybe he does and maybe he doesn't," said Buck.

"Leastwise," I said, "since I've rode this far into the deal with you, I think that you might open up and tell me what's what so far as you know."

"Kid," he answered, "there's nothing I appreciate more than the way that you've kept yourself from pestering me with questions on this here trip. I thought that my tongue would ache just from saying, I don't know. But you've kept your face shut. Now I'll tell you why I ain't talked out more free and easy to you . . . and the reason is that, although you're my pal, I've given my word that I won't talk no more than I have to."

"They've made you swear to keep things as dark as possible?"

"That's what they've done, though they must've known that they was taking a chance."

"They were," I said, "seeing that your wagon ain't any ghost wagon. If a blind man wanted to follow you, he would have an easy time of it."

"He would," said Buck, "but he would have to take along provisions for several days, I guess."

That was true, too. The best way to discourage anybody that started on that trail would just be to let him taste some of the length of the miles and the length of the hot days.

How the mules got through it I can't guess. I know that my Jupe, who was about as tough as they come in any country, was fagged and almost done for. But those mules had grain twice a day from the sacks that big Buck Logan carried along with him. And every time he came to a suspicion of a run of water, Buck would stop the team and drench them down, sloshing the water over them for an hour at a time, because he said that did them a lot of good.

He made three halts a day: in the midmorning, a long one at noon, and another in the middle of the long afternoon. And heaven knows how long a hot afternoon can be in the desert. Every time he halted, he would strip every peg and strap of harness from the mules, and he would wash off the sweat from their shoulders and the backs of their necks where the heavy collars galled them, and then he would turn them loose to graze on whatever grass that they could find and to enjoy a roll and a mite of freedom, at least.

Of course it took a lot of time, and it cost him more work than you would ever guess, because he had to do it all himself. Those mules didn't appreciate the touch of any human being other than Buck, and I think he was proud of having such a string of man-eaters and wanted to keep them just that way.

But the way they ate up the miles, and the way they snaked that heavily loaded wagon through the drift sands was a caution. Half a dozen times we had to get out and shovel out trenches through the loose surface and down to the hard footing for them. But every other time they worked their own way out in a very scientific fashion.

They got thin, but they stuck to their jobs, and they were still in amazingly good shape when the gray head of the leader turned through the little pass between the hills and we saw the green of the valley beneath us—Daggett Valley—and it never could have looked better, even to the gold rushers, than it did to us.

There was a boundary that you could cross in three steps, most of the way. On one side of the hills everything was dead and burned. And on the other side the sand hills showed you what they would grow when they had a fair chance to get a drink of water now and then. So that it was a pretty sight, I can tell you, with the grass growing as thick and as even and as crowded as though it had been planted.

Buck couldn't resist the temptation. He unharnessed his team right there, and we watched them break into those green fields and eat and eat, and then stop to roll, and then get up and eat again like gluttons. You couldn't've trusted a dry-fed horse with such fodder; he would've killed himself, sure. But a mule is different; it is too mean to do itself any real harm. Well, those mules feasted themselves full, and we sat down and drank in the beauty of the valley, and I'll tell you how soft we were. When a fat young buck stepped out of the brush to watch the mules playing with one another, neither Buck Logan nor myself reached for a rifle. We just felt plumb peaceful.

And, for that minute, I forgot that I was riding into danger of some kind about which I knew nothing, as yet. However, things that begin well don't always have the best endings.

V

We didn't make any effort to forge ahead again that day. We rested, and the horse and mules rested. Bright and early the next morning, we started down the valley.

The sun was burning hot, but the minute we got among the trees everything was cool and pleasant. I never saw finer pines in my life.

We pushed up the old road that followed along beside the creek. I think we went about a mile when we heard the clinking of hammers ahead of us, and, when the mules were given a halt and a breathing space, the trees were filled with echoes flying about as the hammers chattered away. It was almost like the noises that you wake up and hear in a town. I looked at Buck Logan.

However, he didn't choose to talk, and I wouldn't ask questions, but I knew that was our goal—that place where men were busy building. And I was glad of it. There was something cheerful about the sound; it did you good to listen to it.

Then we started ahead again, and we came out from under the shadows of the big pines and into a clear stretch with only a scattering of trees here and there. On a hillside near the creek was not a camp being built, but a big house.

It was a good, strongly built house, big enough to have maybe a dozen rooms in it, and I could guess that it must have been run up back in the days of the mining boom, when perhaps the creek looked good enough to one of the miners to be home all the year around.

Indeed, I think that some of those miners thought that the pay dirt would never give out. They got so many quick millions out of the surface dirt that they thought there had to be a continuation down into the rocks. It was too good to finish off with nothing—but, strangely, that was exactly what happened.

The gold was gutted out of the creek. Nothing was left but the bare rigs of the rocks and the big trees. In a single month the whole population drifted away. I had never known there was such a house as this up the creek. But, for that matter, there was a whole lot about the creek and the creek people that nobody ever knew for certain. For a couple of years a thousand things happened every day along that little run of water. There were enough murders and excitement of all kinds to fill a book every week. One thing piled on top of the other, and the heads of people were too filled to retain everything.

However, there was the house as big as life, and the clattering of the hammers came from inside of it. Out in front there was a litter of lumber and some home-made sawbucks, with a drift of yellow sawdust lying on the ground and sparkling almost like the glittering gold itself.

I didn't need more than that to explain everything. The last eight-mule load of lumber had gone to this same spot, and the carpenters were using up the last of it to fix up the inside of the house, while Buck Logan brought on more stuff to polish off the job. That was enough explanation for any man. I mean that was enough surface explanation, though underneath the surface there was as much of a mystery as ever. Why people would want to come out here to the end of the world, beat me.

I soon learned that the two carpenters who had been so busily at work were Roger Beckett and Zack Morgan. And I learned, also, that it was to be my job to guard the house against intruders. But how was I to go about guarding the place, since that was my duty?

I talked it over with big Buck Logan. My idea was that I should stand guard with guns at hand all day and only knock off for a short sleep at night. It would be hard work, but at the same time it would be some return for the high pay that I was getting. Buck listened to all I had to say, and then he simply smiled at me. He said that it showed my heart was right, but it showed that I was not thinking very straight.

How could I stand guard and shelter the whole house, and the men working here and there all around the place, and the inside and outside? I could stand guard for a year and have a thousand men shot down around me from the shelter of the trees that overlooked the house on all sides.

Yes, that was very true, and I could see it, so I asked Buck to make his own suggestions. He had some, of course. There was never a man to beat Buck for suggestions; he had more ideas than an east wind has drops of rain. He said that the main thing was for me to take it easy and have a good time.

"How can I sit around and take it easy," I said, "when I got the responsibility of the lives of three gents on my hands, and half a dozen murderers waiting out yonder . . . as you tell me there are . . . all ready to jump in and cut our throats?"

Buck, he only smiled at me. He said: "Now, kid, don't go off half-cocked, like this. Lemme tell you something that is true and damned true at that. Nobody can really work well until he can work happily, and the picture of you standing up and holding onto a gun all day long ain't a happy picture. I tell you what you do. You like hunting. Now what you should do is to make this a little hunting party. You can't have your eyes open all day and every day, and all night and every night. What I say is that you should just go out and look for game two or three times a day. And when you go out regular for game, what always happens? The game is scared away. Well, kid, you can bet your boots that this two-legged game that we're talking about will be scared away, too . . . or, at least, it will get damn' cautious. It will see signs of your tramping around this here place in a big circle. And it will make them pretty cautious.

"Now, what I'd suggest is that you go out about three times . . . and that you pick the times when folks generally start out on deviltry. They go out in the morning, in the half light, to commit a lot of their crimes. And then they go out in the evening again. And besides that, of course, the time that they like best of all is the night. So I suspect that you'd better make a round in the mornings. Just loop around through the trees and zigzag so that you cover a couple of miles, keeping your eyes open all of the time. After that you take your time off and loaf along until the evening. And when the evening comes, you can make another trip, and the same sometime during the night."

"Look here, Buck, you want me to go hunting at night?"

"I'm not asking you to hunt painters or 'coons," said Buck. "All I'm asking you to do is to ward off men from us, and if it's hard for you to see at night, it will be hard for them, too. I've an idea that you might have a lot more luck by night than you have by day."

This gave me something to think about. But, after all, it wasn't very hard to see that Buck, as usual, was pretty right. If I stood around with a gun all day long, what would I be except a mark for them to shoot at? But if I traipsed around through the forest in the evening and in the morning—that is to say, in the hunting times when all the beasts turn out in the woods—then it would be a good deal different. I might have luck.

I said: "Here's another little thing. Suppose I do come across somebody. What do I do?"

"Shoot," said Buck. "Do I have to tell you that?"

"Shoot without any warning given?" I said.

"Why the devil should you give a warning?"

"Buck," I replied, "I see that you got an idea that I'm just a butcher . . . which I ain't at all. Gents have got to be warned away from this valley before they're shot down, and how is this to be arranged?"

"You're getting so particular, kid," said Buck, "that I dunno how you're going to be useful. What chance is there of anybody but crooks being stirring around here?"

"Not much chance," I admitted.

"Not one chance in a million," Buck said. "No, sir, and you know that. Whoever comes here to the Daggett Valley? Since the last of the gold was washed out, nobody comes here. You couldn't find a man here with a fine-toothed comb, except for the throat-cutters that would like to get rid of the whole mob of us. So you're just talking through your hat uncommon loud and long, old son."

Well, there was a good deal in what he said. I thought it all over and I asked him how far the property ran that his boss—the folks that owned the old house on the hill—had a claim to in the valley. Buck pointed out the boundaries to me. It was a right smart piece of land, too, I can tell you.

I mapped out a regular beat for myself. The first time I made the round, I spent a lot of time setting out the signs on which I had made up my mind. Those signs were flat, thin pieces of big board that I nailed onto trees where they could be seen easy, and on every board there were a few words in black paint:

PRIVATE PROPERTY
NO TRESPASSING

That was a sign that I could remember seeing and hating when I was a boy, because it had always looked sort of poisonous and mean, you know. But I figured that, with those signs up, there would be a lot more excuse for me if I was to turn loose and pepper any strangers with powder and lead.

Buck, he let me do all of these things, and he agreed with me that it was the best way, and that it was making our game more aboveboard.

When I had finished putting up those signs and making my rounds, it was a good first day's work, and I was satisfied. I had stuck up about a dozen of those boards at all of the most prominent places, so that it would be pretty near impossible for folks that followed any of the natural trails toward the old house to fail to see those signs and read the warning that was on them. It was my duty, as near as I could make out. When I had done that, I had another talk with Buck and Zack Morgan, and Roger Beckett. They all three agreed with me that from that time on, if I found any folks inside of the limits of those signs, I wouldn't have to stop and ask any questions. I could just haul off, and turn loose on them, and drop them if I could.

Besides, you see that the ground that I had fenced off with my warnings wasn't all of the property that belonged to the owner of the house, according to Buck Logan. It really wasn't more than a quarter or a fifth of the whole layout. But even so, it was big enough to make a stiff walk three times each twenty-four hours.

When I started making these rounds, things settled down at once. The two gents who were working at the repairing of the house, their nerves got quieter. You would think that I hadn't just started walking my rounds—you would think that I had fenced in that place with a wall of brass half a mile high.

VI

I was getting ready for my morning round, several days later, when Buck Logan came down to me, his face yellowed and covered with wrinkles and shadows around his eyes, like a man who hasn't slept for weeks.

He said: "This is the big day, Doc."

"All right," I said. "If this is the big day, tell me what my part in it is to be."

"Get your Jupe horse," said Buck, "and start drifting over toward the edge of the valley . . . the same road that we come in by. Go to that road and wait there till you see a covered wagon coming . . . an old-fashioned schooner. When you see that, ride up to it. You'll find a little gent with a pointed gray beard driving, and along with him there'll be an old gent with long white hair and a tolerable pretty girl. You ride right up to them and likely you'll have a gun held onto you, but don't be scared by that. It'll simply mean that the gent with the gray beard is playing safe. You go on up with your hands over your head and say that I sent you to him."

"What name shall I call him?" I asked.

"Names ain't any matter," Buck Logan answered. "You don't need no names. Just give my name when you come up, and that'll be enough. But after that, mind that you don't do too much talking."

"All right," I said, "I can get along without talking. But what am I to do about the wagon and the folks that are in it?"

He said: "Your job is to get that wagon safe down through the trees and up the valley to the house, here. You understand?"

"I understand," I said.

"And one of the main things is for you to make sure you don't get it here before sunset. You hear?" He counted out these things with a frown, stabbing at the palm of his hand with his forefinger.

I nodded. I couldn't make out why the wagon had to get to the old house after sunset time, but then that went along with a flock of other things that I didn't understand. I was getting used to being in a sort of a mist. I had, in all my time there, learned that the chief one from whom we expected a lot of trouble was named Grenville.

"Does Grenville want to stop that wagon?" I asked Buck.

He shook his head. "I dunno," he said. "Maybe Grenville does, and maybe he don't. Just what goes on inside of his head, I can't make out, but, if he does suspect what those folks mean to us, he'll make the biggest try in the world to stop the rig. You understand?"

I nodded.

"I mean, he'll try killing," said Buck Logan.

"All right," I said. "The three of you stay here. I go out to bring in a wagon where there's a girl, a white-haired old man, and only one gent able to use guns . . . and him no youngster, as far as I can make out. I may have the whole gang of Grenville on my back."

Buck nodded again. "Of course you may," he said. "There's no doubt about that. You're playing a dangerous game, today. But I'll tell you what . . . I'd almost as soon have your job at the wagon as have you away from the house this morning. If Grenville don't hit at you and the folks on the wagon, he's pretty apt to hit at me and the boys that are here."

He seemed pretty serious about it, and Buck was not of a nature to take trouble any more serious than it had to be taken.

"All right, Buck," I said, "this is the beginning of the big play, then?"

"The beginning of the big play," he said, still as solemn as an owl.

"So long," I said.

"So long," Buck replied, and turned on his heel.

So I went and got my Jupe and rode down the valley. I was so glad that the misery was gonna be over, danger or no danger, that I could have sung, and I did sing, as I went ramping along, as though there was not the least mite of danger in the world from Grenville and his clan.

This was the way I was feeling then—pretty proud and pretty happy—as I worked my way down through the woods, keeping to the old wagon trail, and not making any particular effort to keep Grenville or any of his look-outs from spotting me.

When I look back to it, I wonder how any man could have been so plumb foolish as I was, when I started out. As if I hadn't been warned enough. No, you would think I had never been in that valley before, and that I didn't know there was such a person as Grenville in the whole wide world.

Well, we came to the place on the trail where there had been a bridge, but the bridge that crossed the old gully had busted down, long ago, and the wreckage of the woman that had busted it down lay there in the hollow. The heavy ironwork of the wagon, that hadn't been washed away in the spring freshets, had lodged among the rocks. The trail itself had swung aside, instead of rebuilding the wrecked bridge. The trouble had happened, I suppose, along toward the end of the mining days when it was hardly worthwhile repairing the road.

Anyway, the road dipped to the side and across the gulch at a slant, and just as we got to the middle of the crossing, while I was watching the ground ahead of me, Jupe stopped and whirled to the side. I thought the old fool was refusing on account of a little patch of water, an inch or so deep, that lay in front of us. So I cursed him and give him the spur—but, instead of straightening out, he just threw up his head with a snort. As he threw it up, a gun banged from the thicket, and the bullet that was meant for my brain pashed through Jupe's.

VII

At least, poor Jupe died without pain. He fell so sudden and complete that I didn't have time to free my feet from the stirrups. Also, I think that the quickness of that fall saved my life a second time.

That fellow in the bushes was shooting as straight as he was shooting fast. One bullet combed past my head as Jupe fell, and another spattered dirt in my face as I rolled out of the saddle along the ground. That roll carried me within twisting distance of the brush, and I pitched myself into it just as a fourth bullet came whining for me.

I knew, as I crawled through those bushes, that only fate and Jupe had saved me. And kneeling there in the brush, handling my guns, I knew, too, that in five minutes either I would be dead for sure, or the gent that had tried to murder me would be eating dirt.

I started straight for him. Yes, I was so mad that I went smashing and crashing through the brush, aiming right for the spot from which he had done the shooting—as though he must have used up his bullets, or as though I couldn't be killed with powder and lead. Anyway, my wits came back to me before I had gone very far. I stopped on the edge of a little depression that couldn't be very far away from the spot where the other gent had lain for me. There was a part of a rotten stump lying on the ground in front of me, and I kicked that stump so that it rolled along down the slope and came to rest in the brush straight ahead of me. There it lay, and it had made a sound a good deal like that which a man makes in charging wild, through the woods.

So I thought if the other gent really was near, the noise of that rolling stump might make him think I had ducked down into the brush at the bottom of that dip of ground. Leastwise, if he was thinking that, there was nothing to keep me from taking him from behind.

I went slithering along as soft as I was able to work, and thanking heaven for the breeze that come rustling and talking through the tops of the trees. That wind made about enough sound to drown out all the noise I was making. So I worked myself in a circle that brought me through a thick standing hedge of young poplars. And then my heart jumped into my throat, for there he was, stretched out along the ground and turned away from me, with his rifle at the ready, trained on something before him and beneath him. I knew he was searching the hollow into which I had rolled the bit of stump.

I raised up easy and stepped through the trees.

I didn't want to take advantage of him, and so I figured that if I put my Colt into the holster and called out a warning to him, it would make about an even thing of it—his rifle against the surprise that I was giving him.

I did just that. I sneaked my revolver back into the holster, but just as I did that, something seemed to pop into his head and make him uneasy, because all at once he lifted up his head and stiffened all through his body.

"You hound dog!" I snarled at him through my teeth. I was thinking of the way that poor old Jupe had died for me—and just then it looked to me as though no man's life was more than enough to be paid down for that little old cutting horse of mine.

When he heard my voice, he pitched himself right around and snatched his gun to his shoulder. I was half of a mind that, when he heard a voice like that behind him, he would stick up his hands, but there wasn't any quit in that man. He started for me like I was nothing at all, and almost before I could wink, the long barrel of that rifle was flashing at my eyes.

I yanked out my Colt. I didn't have time to take any aim or draw any bead. It was just a case of a snap shot from the hip, in case I wanted to get in something before he planted me with an aimed bullet. I fired from the hip the instant I had flipped my Colt out.

The shot hit the gravel just in front of him and brought out a yell and a gasp. His rifle went off, but the bullet rattled through the branches, a long distance away from me. He jumped to his feet and threw his hands across his face. He was blinded a bit. And, instead of shooting him down, I thought that it might be a pretty good thing if I closed in on him and took him a prisoner—because then he could act as a sort of hostage for us and maybe keep Grenville from trying to murder us from behind the brush. So I ran in at him, full of this new idea.

It would have been easy, if he had really been blinded, but he wasn't. He saw me coming and wrenched at his Colt. He got it out of the holster, but just then I reached for him with my fist and managed to hit his jaw. He went down on his back with a thump and a grunt, and his Colt clanged on the rocks.

No, he wasn't done fighting yet. As he lay there, he kicked out and knocked my feet out from under me. Down I fell right on top of him, and, believe me, it was like falling on the top of a wildcat. He was just a mite faster than chain lightning and a little bit stronger than a tiger. But as I fell, I got a throat hold. He whanged at my face, and he tore at my hands. He was so strong that in half an instant he was on top of me, and I was under him. But before he could use that advantage, my grip told on him. His face blackened, his eyes turned up in his head, and he went limp and soft.

I rolled him off and threw a handful of water in his face from my canteen. And I saw him come to by steps and stages, as you might say, just pulling himself together by degrees, so I sat up and shook myself to see where I was hurt.

I can tell you that had been an exciting little whirl, while it lasted, but when I had gathered myself together, there was the chap sitting up and beginning to blink at me. I blinked at him, too, and I was terrible surprised by what I saw, because here was the red hair and the fine, handsome features that I had been told Red Grenville had.

"Look here," I said, "are you any relation of Henry Grenville?"

"Perhaps I am," he answered, as he began to brush the leaves and the dirt out of his hair, as cool as you please.

"Well," I said, "I was half of a mind that I would take you along with me, alive. Now that I see that you come of decent blood, and that you should know better than to shoot from cover . . . why, curse you . . . I got a mind to plant a slug between your eyes and leave you here."

He smiled straight into my face. There was a ton of nerve in him.

"How long," he asked, "have gunfighters like you been in the habit of talking about fair play and not shooting from cover?"

It was a facer for me. I listened, and I wanted to shoot him full of holes, I can tell you, but I managed to control myself. I don't know how. I said to him: "I'll tell you, old-timer, that wherever you've learned your stuff about me, you've learned it wrong."

"Bah!" he said. "How many men have you shot down from behind a wall? And how many have you shot through the back?"

I let out a yell, it made me so mad. "You young fool!" I shouted at him. "If I shot men from behind, why didn't I shoot you down that way, when I had the chance to take you helpless from behind, just now, instead of giving you a little more than a fair break for your life?"

"Why . . . ," he began, and then he stuck.

In the excitement of things happening so fast and so close together, I suppose he had not had a chance to think things over exactly as they happened. Now he frowned and looked as though this thing he had just thought about made him a little unhappy.

"I don't care about that," he said rather sullenly. "The fact is that Henry has told us that you're worthy to be hunted like a dog . . . and that's my excuse . . . and that's excuse enough."

"Henry Grenville told you that?"

53

"Yes," he said. "I suppose that you'll call him a liar?"

I didn't answer. I saw that there was no use in arguing with him over a thing like this. The main thing was that I had a brother of Henry Grenville that I could use as a sort of hostage. And I could just about swear that Henry would stop the shooting from behind trees, from this point on.

"Stand up," I ordered. "Stand up and get ready to march."

"I'm ready here," he said. "I'd as soon pass out here as anywhere, but I don't think that I'll march for you."

VIII

It took me a moment or so to understand that this young fool had it fixed in his mind that I was going to murder him before I got through.

When I had digested that idea for a minute, I looked him in the eye, and I said: "Grenville, what's your first name?"

"Lawrence," he said as cool as ever.

"Lawrence," I said, "lemme tell you that your brother may be a blooming angel so far as truth-telling may be concerned, and I may be the worst black rat in the world, but the fact is, old-timer, that I ain't going to murder you. Not today, that is. Maybe tonight I'll cut your throat, or maybe tomorrow I'll shoot you through the back, but, today, I've taken a fancy to letting you live, y'understand? And if you care to eat a couple of more squares, you'll buck up and do what I tell you. But, if the next few hours ain't got nothing in store for you, why . . . I'll polish you off right here and now."

He listened to me as though I was speaking a foreign language that he didn't understand. But finally he said: "Well, I'll let you have it your own way. Where do you want me to march to?"

"Where I tell you," I answered, and I guided him back through the woods to the spot where

55

my poor Jupe lay. I said: "This is what you done, Larry, my boy."

"He threw his head up," Grenville said, cool as a cucumber. "Otherwise you'd be lying there, and he'd be eating grass . . . with an empty saddle."

I couldn't help admiring this young fool of a boy in a way. Nobody but a courageous idiot, that didn't care whether or not he lived, would talk like this to a man who had the drop on him. But it was plain to be seen that courage ran pretty thick in the blood of the Grenvilles.

I said: "Yes, you meant that bullet for me, but maybe, while you were shooting at me, you murdered something that was a lot better than me . . . if you admit that a horse can be better than a man."

"Ah," he said, with a quick look aside at me, "don't I admit that, though? I do. And I've known the horses . . . and the men." And he laughed with a sudden sort of enthusiasm.

I began to take more and more of a liking for him. Even if he had been taught to shoot from behind trees—well, there was something decent about him in spite of that.

"Look here, Grenville," I said, "this here Jupe was the best cutting horse I ever rode on. And he was the gamest horse on the trail that you ever seen."

"He's a pretty little rabbit," Grenville admitted.

"Rabbit?" I repeated. "That rabbit, you bonehead, would carry two hundred pounds at a canter nearly all day long. He's stood between me and a rotten sort of a death more times than once. Do you think that the fact that he died for me makes me feel any easier about it, or any kinder to you, Grenville?"

All the time that I said this he wasn't looking at the horse, he was looking at me, and, when I finished, he said: "Willis, if I'd been you . . . well . . . Larry Grenville would be a dead man."

"Well," I replied, "there was never a time from the beginning of the world when shooting from behind brush done any real good. It's got me a dead horse, and I think that you're decent enough to have it give you a few bad nights during the rest of your life. Now help me get the saddle off of him."

He started to work without a word. We stripped everything off of Jupe, and then he pointed to a tower of loose rocks that heaved up on the bank just above the spot where Jupe lay in the hollow. I took that for a pretty good hint, and we heaved away side-by-side until that tower toppled, and three or four tons of rocks went crashing and sliding over the spot where Jupe was and buried him from sight completely.

After that it was easier to go along on my trail, but Larry was a pretty silent boy for the rest of the way. He didn't have anything to suggest, and his head hung pretty low.

But suddenly he broke out, as we turned onto the upslope that pointed toward the edge of the valley: "Henry was all wrong about you, Willis."

"I'll tell you why," I said. "I would be a lot more use to him dead than living. You can write that down for fact. Step out, kid . . . I'm overdue."

We swung down that trail for another couple of miles, until we came to the edge of the green, and there was the whiteness and the oven heat of the desert before us.

"What d'you aim to do with me?" asked Larry Grenville.

"I aim to keep you with me," I said, "as a sort of a promise that, while you're here, Henry won't try his hand at any more Indian fighting. Is that fair?"

He nodded right away. "That's fair," he said.

"And if you try to break away . . . why, I'll treat you the way you treated my little old Jupe. Is that square?"

"The squarest thing in the world," he said. "And damn it, Willis, I feel as though this was a black day in my life." And he went on with a frown on his face, thinking hard all of the time.

We kept on for about another hour, and then I made a halt on the edge of one of the low sand hills where we could get at something that served as an excuse for shade—I mean, we sat down in the skeleton shadow of a group of Spanish daggers. And we let the perspiration come trickling down our faces while I stared off to the horizon across the flashing and shining heat waves of the desert.

By what big Buck Logan had said, I had guessed that I would find the covered wagon coming over the hills early in the morning, but it was pretty near to noon before I saw a little spot of white against the sky, like a cloud brushing across the face of the earth.

"What's that?" asked Larry.

"More trouble for your brother is what it looks like to me," I told him.

He stared and started, but he wouldn't ask any more questions.

Finally I said: "Look here, Larry, do you know the thing that brought your brother up here to Daggett Valley?"

"Of course," he said with a quick look to the side at me.

"Is it worth the trouble that he's taking?" I asked.

"That all depends," Lawrence Grenville said. "The money might be worth the trouble to him, but the fun would be worth the trouble to me."

"And do the gents that are working for Henry figger on getting in on a split of the loot?"

"They work by the day," Larry answered, "but why do you ask me this stuff?"

"I wanted to see," I said, "how big a business-man he was."

The dust cloud was floating along across the hills toward us, and now that cloud lifted a little, and I could see through the film of it the outlines of the arched back of the wagon, and then four animals pulling the load. It couldn't be a very heavy load, because they came along at a fast walk. They did not stop at the inclines, as Buck Logan had stopped his mule team when he worked our way across the same trail.

Now it came closer and closer. It was one of those old-fashioned wagons such as they used to use, in the gold days, for making voyages around on the prairie and across the barren desert.

Grenville stood up and peered at them. "It looks odd," he said. "What are they doing with one of those clumsy old things?"

"Why," I said, "maybe they're on the track of the same trouble that brought your brother into Daggett Valley. Come on down with me, and we'll hail them."

He stepped out from the shadow along with me, but as we got down onto the trail there was a shout from in front of us. I saw the mules stop, and I saw a rifle leveled at us in the hands of a man with a gray, pointed beard.

Buck was a true mind-reader, right enough.

IX

"You've walked us into a bunch of lead," Larry Grenville said. "I thought you were a friend of this gang?"

It was a fact. The gray-bearded fellow looked pretty wicked behind that rifle of his, but we hoisted up our hands and walked in to talk to the tiger, face to face. When we got to the heads of the leading span of mules, he stopped us again.

"Now who are you?" he asked me.

"I am Doc Willis," I told him.

He snapped: "Where's your horse?"

"Dead," I said.

"Dead where?"

"Dead in Daggett Valley," I said.

"And you walked on here?"

"Yes."

"With good news or bad?"

"With no news worth talking about," I said.

"Keep your hands up," he said, "and let your partner back up a bit."

I told Grenville to do as he was ordered, and he backed out of the way, while the gray beard climbed down from his seat and came up to me. As soon as he was on the ground, he didn't look half so impressive as sitting down. He was one of those short-legged, long-waisted fellows.

I suppose he didn't stand taller than me, but, seated, he looked like a six-footer, at least. He came toward me with a sort of a wobble in his stride, because he was very bow-legged.

"Now," he said, speaking quietly when he came up to me, "tell me where you stand . . . and you don't have to shout it."

I said: "Buck Logan sent me out here to meet you."

"To meet who?" he said.

"A girl, a white-haired old gent, and a gray-bearded fellow in a covered wagon."

"And what names did Buck tell you they wore?"

"Buck told me no names."

He frowned again at this. "What did Buck mean by that?" he growled.

"You can answer that better than me," I said.

"What's your job with Buck?" he asked me.

"Me? I'm the chore boy, and I carry water for the real men."

"Don't talk smart," said the gray-bearded gent. "That will win you nothing with me. I asked you what you were doing for Buck."

"Fifty dollars' worth a week," I said.

He canted his head a little to one side. "Buck is paying big wages, then," he said.

"That's all in the way you look at it," I told him. "It looked good to me at first, but now it looks fairly small."

"Humph!" he said.

"Humph!" I responded.

"Bear a civil tongue in your head," he said. "Do you know who I am?"

"I don't give a damn who you are," I said. "A gray beard ain't a title, not in this part of the world."

I thought that that would get a flare out of him, but instead he let a smile come halfway on his lips.

"You don't get fifty a week for that sort of talk," he said.

"No," I said, "I get fifty a week for riding herd on the rest of them and keeping the chills away."

"Humph!" he said again. "Then you're the killer that Logan was to try to hook up with?"

"Am I the killer?" I said, getting madder and madder. "Well, in my part of the country folks ain't so fond of calling me that."

"Oh," he said, "I'll be polite to you, if that's what you want. And what was your name again?"

"Willis," I said, and, as I looked him over, I felt that there wasn't anybody that I ever had met that I liked less than this fellow. He was about as cold as ice, and his eyes had a way of going right through you and finding out what was on your insides.

"Willis," he said, "you came out to guide us into the valley, I suppose, but you don't know who I am?"

"I don't," I admitted. "And I don't . . ."

"Leave that out," he broke in, as cool as ever, but smiling a little again. "But you might as well know me now . . . I'm Alston."

"Alston?" I repeated. "Then I suppose that the old white-headed gent on the seat, yonder, is Carberry?" For I'd heard some mention of a gent by the name of Carberry being mixed up in this affair.

He gave a start and a blink. "Carberry? Why, don't you know . . . ," began Alston. Then he stopped himself and stared at me, like a man would at a fellow who said that the earth was flat.

"No," I said, "I never had the pleasure of meeting up with Carberry. Who is he? President?"

"Maybe you'll be ready to vote for him in that job," the gray beard said, "before you get through with this game. Now, who is the fellow who's with you?"

"Don't you like him?" I asked.

"Don't be sassy, Willis," Alston said. "Tell me who he is. I have a right to know, because I won't take another step into the valley without knowing who I have along with me."

"All right," I replied to him, "I don't mind telling you that he is the gent that dropped my Jupe horse."

He took another quick look at young Larry Grenville, and then he took a long look at me and seemed to be really seeing me for the first time. "The man who killed your horse . . . how?"

"From behind a tree."

"And you got him?"

"There he is."

"But you didn't scalp him, eh?"

"Alston," I said, continuing to get madder and madder, "whether you like the looks of me, or I like the looks of you ain't a matter of any importance. What really counts is that I ain't a killer, and that I won't be talked to like one. And I want you to write that down in red letters and never to forget it. I don't kill gents for the sake of keeping my hand in."

"Very hot," Alston said, nodding at me and looking me over like I was a horse or a dog. "All right. I won't rub your hair the wrong way. Only . . . what do you intend to do with the man? What's his name?"

"Grenville," I answered.

I thought that might get a little more attention from him, but I didn't expect it to make him stagger. He reached out and gripped my arm, and there was a lot more power in that hand of his than I had thought. By the feel of that grip of his, I peeled ten years off my guess at his age. No, he wasn't as old as the gray beard had made him look—not by a long ways.

"Henry Grenville?" he said. "That's not possible. And yet . . . I can half remember the face, and there is the red hair. Good heavens, Willis, if that's Grenville, our troubles are all ended."

"Are they?" I snarled at him, because I hated him every minute more and more. "Well, he's Grenville, all right, but his first name isn't Henry."

"Not Henry? The devil!"

I told him that the name of this fellow was Lawrence, but here Alston pricked up his ears again. He said that next to having Henry himself, this capture was best because, with it, we could tie the hands of Henry himself pretty effectually. He said that we would put Larry into the wagon, and that he, Alston, would keep guard over him, while the old chap drove the wagon along the road, and I went on ahead to scout for trouble.

"Because," Alston explained, "when Henry finds out that his brother has disappeared, he'll come shouting for trouble, and when he starts to make trouble, he's very apt to finish the job that he begins." Then he took me back toward the wagon. "Don't mind the old boy," he said. "He's pretty safe and sane, today. But I had a rocky time with him on Wednesday."

While he led me up toward the seat, we took another look around for Larry. I hadn't been watching him very close, because it would be hard for him to get away. He had no gun with him, now, and, if he tried to break away, it would be dead easy for me to pick him off before he had got very far through that loose surface of sand.

Well, there hadn't been any idea in the mind of Larry of escaping. And now there he was, leaning beside the driver's seat, as calm as you please, smoking away at a cigarette and making conversation with the old fellow and the girl.

They made a picture, I can tell you, Larry Grenville, almost handsomer than any man had a right to be, standing there with his head thrown back, and the girl leaning above him and laughing down to him—and she prettier than any I had ever seen. The old chap, he sat back with his hands folded in his lap, smiling at Larry, and smiling at the girl, but with his eyes mostly fixed far off on the horizon, and his smile not meaning a great deal of anything. I could see that he was only about half or a quarter with us. Sickness and death had begun at the top with him. And when I came up close and looked up into his thin, kind, old face, with the white hair streaming down around it, a wave of pity came over me that I've never recovered from to this day. I would have cut off an arm to make the old chap smile with a bit of life in his face.

Alston did the introducing in a pretty free and easy way.

"Lou Wilson," he said to the girl, "this is Willis. And, Doc, this is William Daggett."

I had thought there couldn't be many more surprises crowded into this day of my life. From the beginning right straight, there had been something happening every little while, but this was the crown of everything, for here was a name that had passed from reality and become part of a story, all through that section of the West. Here was the man that had struck gold on the creek. Here was the man that had struck the gold and started the rush that crowded Daggett Creek, in a little while, with miners gouging through the earth to get rich. Here was the man, too, who had built the house on the hill that Buck had been working so hard to get into shape and freshen up and make like new.

And what was he? Why, the man that had done all of these things and made so much history, he was just a hollow husk. Once there had been a man inside of him, but now he was like a light that has burned low and is about to flicker out. And there was a flicker in the blue eyes of Daggett, as he smiled down at me—a quiet, sad, feeble sort of a light that made me almost sorry that I was alive.

"I'm proud to know you, Mister Daggett," I said. "I've just been up in the valley where you . . ."

Here Alston stepped heavily on my foot. But I hadn't made any break, so far as the old fellow was concerned. He just smiled and nodded at me and said: "Exactly. Exactly. And what a world it is, Mister Wallis."

Even my name, which he'd heard half a minute before, he couldn't remember; and now his old blue eyes wandered off to find their favorite spot on the horizon.

X

Alston wanted for me to handle the team while he watched Grenville in the wagon. I said that I would, but not being used to handling four reins, I jumped up onto the near-leader and started to guide the team that way, reining the leaders the way I wanted them to go. But before we had rolled a hundred yards, somebody yipped on the far side of the off-leader, and there was Lou Wilson, sitting sidewise on the off-leader, and laughing at me, as easy and as companionable as you please.

I looked back to the wagon, and it amused me a good deal to see that it bothered two of them a lot to watch the girl out there riding the mule at my side. It bothered young Larry Grenville, for one. And it bothered the gray beard, too.

Lou hooked a thumb back over her shoulder. "How did you ever happen to pick up with this gang of thugs?" she asked.

"I was gonna ask you the same thing," I said.

"You were?" Lou said. "Well, I asked you first. Let's have what you got to say for yourself."

"Suppose," I said, "that you were a cow-puncher."

"Yes," she said.

"And suppose that you were out of a job, and

wondering what gang you would pick on with next, and suppose the most you ever got for riding range was about forty bucks a month . . ."

"I know," she said.

"And then a gent drives by with an eight-mule load of lumber and he says . . . 'Come along with me and get your fifty bucks a week, and all you got to do is to ride herd on a couple of gents that I've got at work.' Why what would you have said, Lou?"

"I would've said . . . 'Come take me quick, before you get a chance to change your mind.' What did you say, Doc?"

"I told him that I didn't want his game, and I let him roll on out of my sight. But after he was gone, I just couldn't stand it. Along in the middle of the day I went pelting along after him, and so . . . here I am, still riding around in circles, and still in the dark."

"In the dark," she repeated with her husky voice suddenly barking at me. "Did I hear you straight?"

"You heard me straight," I told her.

She straightened around so that she could look fairly and squarely at me. It was a strange thing, but when you faced Lou, you could see the thoughts working in her eyes. Not just what they were, of course, but you could see her eyes brighten and darken, and you could see the color change from blue to gray and back again. I never seen such a pair of eyes in my life, and neither did any other man.

"Say, Doc," she said to me, "maybe you're an innocent, poor, young boy that's being dragged into this dirty deal sort of against his will."

"Maybe I am not," I said, laughing back at her when I saw her drift. "I ain't asking you for any of your pity, Lou."

"Thanks," she said. "That's one strain off my mind. But what do you mean by saying that you're riding around in the dark?"

"Ain't that plain English?" I asked.

"Don't get huffy," she said. "I'm not riding you."

"You give a pretty good imitation of it. What are you driving at?"

"You ain't a baby. How could they ring you in with your eyes closed?"

"I'm a hired man, here, not a boss." That seemed to surprise her.

"If they get in gents like you for the hired man rôles," she said, "this is quite a show . . . bigger, even, than I thought."

"And how big did you think?" I asked her.

"Oh, I don't know. Hundreds of thousands, I suppose."

"What makes you suppose that?"

"Are you pumping me?"

"Not a bit more than you want to talk, Lou."

She nodded. It was easy to see that she had her

eyes open all the time, but she didn't want to be hostile. "I don't see any reason why you and I shouldn't be friends, Doc."

"None in the world," I agreed. "I'm keeping a tight hold on myself to keep from being too friendly too quick."

She frowned at me. "What might you mean by that?"

"I'll explain later, when I know you better," I told her.

"Well," said Lou, "have you told me all you know?"

"Oh, no," I said. "I don't mind letting you know what I've gathered. It ain't much."

"Fire away," she said.

"Well, all I know is that Buck Logan brought me up here."

"I've heard about him," she said. "What sort is he?"

"Square," I said. "A big gent, slow-speaking, usually . . . and honest, I think."

"But you ain't sure?"

"I'm sure of nothing in this game."

"Not even of me?"

I looked into those wonderful, queer, changing eyes of hers. "Not even of you."

I thought that this might anger her a little, but there was nothing soft about that girl.

"All right," she said, "that doesn't make me mad. It's gonna be pretty easy to talk to you,

73

Doc. So you don't even know Buck Logan?"

"I don't. I thought I did. I still feel mighty friendly toward him. But lately I've got the idea that this business means a lot more to him than any friendship would."

"No friend would stand between him and the cash he expects to get out of the deal?"

"That's right. That's about the way I figure it."

"Is Logan inside of the deal?"

I thought it over for a minute, then I said: "It seems to me that Logan must know about as much as anybody. But I'm not sure even of that. He may be only a hired man, as far as I know. I'm sure of nothing."

"Go on," she prodded.

"Well, then, I know that up there in the valley there's Henry Grenville, a gentleman with education, and all that. And he's got a crowd of gunfighters with him, and he's gunning to get something out of the deal."

"Is that all you know about him?"

"That's about all. Then there's something about the old Daggett house. Do you know what it is?"

"The Daggett house?" Lou said. "No. What has a house to do with it?"

"A lot. I see that there's a lot you don't know, Lou, but, take it from me, when this thing is opened up and explained, the old Daggett house will have a lot to do with the explanation. At least, that's the way Buck Logan and his crew are expecting it to happen. But they ain't sure. I can see that Buck ain't sure. He's working in the dark, and he don't know just where he's going. And I can see the worry of it in his face all the time."

She nodded, thinking of everything that I had to say.

"Then, behind this thing, or mixed up in it I don't know how, there's you and old Daggett. You can tell me something about that. Then somewhere in the yarn there is Carberry . . ."

"What Carberry?"

"The bandit."

"Carberry, the bandit? Oh, he's dead a long time ago," said Lou.

"Dead!" I shouted at her. "Why, Lou, then his ghost is back in this business and using his hand somewhere and in some way. I know that for certain."

"Go on," said Lou, "this is pretty interesting."

"I've got to the end of my rope," I said. "I used to think, at first, that there was something hidden in the bottom of the house, but, if that was the case, I suppose they would tear the old place to pieces and find out what it was. Anyhow, the thing they're looking for must be so big that it couldn't be hidden in a nutshell, even if it was pure solid gold, it would have to take up a good deal of room."

"Why," Lou said, "maybe they're looking for some sort of a paper."

"Humph!" I said. "That sounds a good deal too much like a book to convince me."

"Maybe it does," she admitted, "but we've got to try everything, if we want to hope to hit on the right trail, here."

I admitted that was right. Then I told her how the old house was being fixed up, and she wondered at that no end. She couldn't make head nor tail out of it, because she agreed with me that nobody would fix up a big house like that just to live in, with Daggett Creek so far from the rest of the world. And what the hidden purpose could be was a sticker.

It was good to talk these things all over with her, because she was as smart as a whip, and she thought three thoughts while I was thinking one. Then I asked her what she knew about Alston, because he seemed to be as high up in the deal as anybody.

She thought for a minute before she answered, and then she said: "Well, I'll tell you about Alston. I've known some crooks in my day. I've known cattle rustlers and yeggs. Dad was free and easy, and he never cared who came and tapped at his door and asked for a meal and a place to sleep. I've seen some pretty hardcases around our house, but I'll tell you what . . . the lowest, the meanest, the sharpest, the smartest,

76

and the wickedest of the lot is that gambler, Alston."

I sort of knew beforehand just what she would say, somehow. I'd felt all of those things about him. So I couldn't help breaking out: "It's pretty good to hear you say that, Lou, because it's easy to see that he don't feel the same way about you as you do about him."

"He wants me to marry him, and he expects that I will, when I see how rich this deal will make him. You understand? But I'll be dead before I ever marry him. You can lay your money on that bet."

Well, that was about the best news I'd ever heard.

XI

I took a while to digest what she'd just told me, and I felt so happy that I couldn't help slapping the mule on the hip and singing out at a rabbit that came hopping across the wagon trail.

"Only," I said at last, "that don't tell me how you were rung in on this deal."

"The reason is back in a bank," said the girl.

"Money?"

"Nothing but. That's why I'm here . . . and a good fat stake."

"I hope so," I told her.

"Twenty-five hundred iron men is what I corralled before I would go along in the party," Lou said.

And I blinked at her. "Why, Lou," I said, "it seems to me that old Alston would hardly pay that much for less than a murder."

"It looks that way, doesn't it?" Lou said. "And now I'll hand you a surprise. He's giving me that money and a lot more, if the deal works, and all for the sake of what?"

"I couldn't guess," I said.

"All for wearing a funny old dress. Can you beat that?"

No, I couldn't beat that, and I was perfectly

willing to tell her so. "All right," Lou said, "but that's the fact, strange though you may think it."

I just looked at her.

"Do you believe me?"

"Lou," I said, "I don't know you well enough to tell you how many kinds of a liar I think you are."

She wasn't mad. She just put back her head and laughed. "Maybe you're partly right, too," she said, "but that's my story, and that is what I've got to stick to."

"Is that part of the bargain with Alston?"

"Alston? No, he'd probably poison you, if he knew that I'd told you even this much."

"Who is Alston?"

"Alston," Lou said, "is a gent that's done what ain't possible."

"How do you mean?"

"In the old days, you know how the gamblers used to come down to the mining camps and cheat the boys out of their gold dust?"

"I've heard about that, and I've seen some of it, of course."

"Well, there's a good old saying that there was never a crooked gambler that didn't go on the rocks sooner or later?"

"Yes."

"Some of them got cleaned out at cards, when they met up with a worse crook than themselves. Some of them got stabbed in the back, and then some of them was shot down in fair fights and . . ."

"That's right, and I've seen it happen."

"But sooner or later, they all go . . . and their money goes, too, because it comes through their hands too easy to stick, you see?"

"All right," I said. "That's all a fact. But what has that to do with Alston?"

"Well, I'll tell you. He's the exception to the rule. He's the one old-time gambler that stayed with the game and that beat it. When he was gambling, he took every chance and played it big . . . big and crooked, I mean to say. He worked cards, and he worked dice. He knew how to fix up a crooked set of horse races and get the money out of the Indians, even. He knew how to salt up a claim very fine and stick a poor sucker with it. He knew all sorts of things . . . but, most of all, he was good at the dice, they tell me. He made money out of everything, and finally he had the nerve to draw back out of the game that he was in and go East and settle down where he could pretend to be respectable. That was the way with this here Alston."

"And now this game has brought him out of his shell?"

"That's it. He's got plenty of money. He's living easy. He's showed me a flock of pictures of his horses, and his dogs, and his house, and all of that. He's terribly proud of it, and it's a pretty good place, right enough. But this deal was big enough for the hopes of what he could make in it to bring him out West. So here he is, and he thinks he'll win . . . though something tells me that he's taking a long, long chance."

"What makes you think that?"

"Why, for one thing, he told me that he never had this idea at all, until he seen me."

That staggered me. "Until he saw you, Lou?" I gasped at her.

"I was in Denver with an uncle of mine. He went to Denver on a trip. And seen me there, and hunted me up, and got to know my uncle . . . just so that he could have a chance to talk to me."

"When was that?"

"Last year."

"Been working on this deal ever since?"

"He said that he couldn't do a thing unless I would promise to work with him. And finally he came across with enough money to make me do what he wanted. And here I am, but that's not the only reason. There's old William Daggett, too. I know that poor old fellow is going to be leaned upon a lot by Alston, and you can see for yourself that Mister Daggett ain't to be depended upon. He's only about half here, and the other half is away off . . . nobody can tell where."

That was right enough.

"And still," I said, "Alston looks like a winner, to me."

"Sure," said Lou. "He says himself that he

wasn't a gambler. He was just a gold digger, but he used cards and such things instead of a pick and shovel and got a lot more of the yellow stuff. He wouldn't be in this deal unless there was a fine big chance that he would win with it."

I looked back into the wagon, and there was Alston sitting steady, with his eyes burning at me. A bit in front of him was Larry Grenville, looking at me about as mean as old Alston was doing.

No, Alston didn't look like a loser—neither did young Grenville, and the two of them worried me a good deal.

"All right," I said to Lou. "There is one pretty sure thing. If Alston is in the deal, it's a crooked one."

"Maybe, and maybe not," said Lou. "I'll think about that when the time comes," and she began to laugh in her husky, careless way. I liked her fine, but she was still a puzzle to me.

I had something to think about besides the stuff of which we had been talking, pretty soon.

While Lou and I exchanged the little mites of information that we had to give, we had been pushing through miles of sand and passed the green borderline just as the sun begun to turn red-gold before falling behind the western mountains. We slid down the first slope, and the leader just brought me over the tip of the next hill—the last hill before we dipped down into the long valley

82

slope—and I had a glimpse, far ahead of me, of a horseman pushing his horse behind a clump of trees.

I didn't ask any questions. I had seen a man, a rifle, and a horse, and I'd been in Daggett Valley long enough to know that that combination was apt to mean pretty ugly business before many hours had rolled by.

I popped off of the mule, and I ran back beside the driver's seat.

"Chief," I said, "there's one man ahead of us in the trees, and, by the way he acts, I figure that he doesn't want to be seen by us. What do we do now?"

"Turn the wagon around," Alston said, "and give the mules the whip."

I stared up at him. He wasn't the sort of a man to give fool advice like that.

He corrected himself right away. "No," he said, "there ain't room to turn it around. We've got to go ahead or stop."

"Stop," I said, "and they'll have a pretty good chance to bag the whole crew of you."

He nodded. His eyes were sparkling and snapping and his lower jaw was thrusting out. "We can't turn around," he said. "If we stop, they eat us up. Could we break through them?"

"They're just beyond the top of the next hill," I told him. "We couldn't get up any speed to drive us over the top of that rise. It don't look big, but it's enough to take all the roll out of our wheels. Besides, the ground is soft over there, and the wheels will cut in too deep. You couldn't keep up a gallop . . . not with just these four mules."

He nodded and swore. "That sounds like the fact," he admitted. "Then there's only one thing left. When the wagon gets down into the hollow, there, it may be that we'll be out of their sight, and, if we are, we got to try to slip out of the wagon and cut away through the trees. Is there much of a chance of that?"

I thought it over. "One poor chance in ten," I told him.

"One chance in ten is the best chance we have, then," he said. "Go get the girl back here into the wagon while I tie the arms of this Grenville."

XII

He kicked on the brakes with his foot, so that the wagon dragged down into the valley, very slow and easy, and that gave us a few more seconds of time.

I ran back to Lou and told her to get down and skin for the wagon.

"What's up?" she asked me, as cool as you please.

"Gents with guns," I said, and waved ahead of me.

"Grenville, I suppose," Lou said, and jumped from the mule and ran back.

When we got there, we found that there was another obstacle that hadn't been planned on. Old William Daggett didn't understand, and there wasn't time to explain.

He said: "Gentlemen, gentlemen . . . if you wish to walk, by all means do so. But I am not very well, and I shall remain with the wagon. It is still some distance to my house, where I hope to make you fairly comfortable. You will pardon me if I don't accompany you on foot."

"Poor old man," Lou said at my ear. "He thinks he's taking us to his house to entertain us. Make Alston be gentle with him."

Alston said: "If I cannot persuade you, I'll have to . . ." And he reached for Mr. Daggett's arm.

I pointed my finger at him like a gun. Well, it stopped him, but he was raving. "Curse you, what is it?" he barked at me.

"Easy with the old boy," I told him.

"All right," Alston said in a fury, jumping down to the ground. "Leave him behind . . . and leave all our hopes behind with him. I tell you, you fool, that we can do nothing without him."

"My dear sirs," old Daggett was saying, blinking at us. "What can it all be about?"

"You try, Lou," I said.

"There's robbers ahead of us, Mister Daggett!" she cried to him.

"Impossible," the old boy replied.

"Oh, we saw them."

"In my valley?" Daggett asked, very severe. "Well, well, I shall have to see to that. The rest of you have no fear. It is my pleasure to protect you . . . and fortunately I am armed." With that he pulled out a little, old snub-nosed gat that must have been thirty years old, and he smiled down at it and then at us. "You see you have nothing to fear," he announced. And there he sat, very tickled to be in at a fight, with the light beginning to glisten in his eyes, and a spot of color growing in his cheeks.

A very fine, noble-looking old fellow. He was the true grit, all right. It sure warmed my heart to watch him as he sat there with that gun shaking and wobbling about in his old hand.

"Of course you're not afraid, Mister Daggett," Lou said, "but we're all afraid. And I'm afraid. You'll come along to take care of me, won't you?"

"God bless me," old Daggett replied. "My dear child, of course I'll come along and take care of you. Of course."

The wagon had about got down to the foot of the slope as the old chap climbed down to the ground, and in an instant we were all of us in the brush.

The mules went on like nothing had happened at all. And the creaking of the wheels and the crushing of the sand and the gravel under the big iron tires made enough noise to cover the sounds that we made as we combed along through the trees.

We had enough encumbrances, though. There was old man Daggett, of course, still with his gun in his hand, telling everybody to hurry on ahead, while he would bring up the rear and take care that no harm overtook the rest of us. And he had to have Alston on one side of him and me on the other, to help him over the rough places and over the creek, because his legs were so stiff and weak and brittle with age and sickness. Then there was young Grenville. Alston was dead set on not letting him get away, and he kept Grenville in his sight all the time and was talking to him, too.

"Grenville," he said, "mind you, that when I shoot, I haven't got blank cartridges in this gun. You hear me talk? And I'll shoot to kill, as sure as you're a foot high."

For my part I believed him, and I could see that Grenville believed him, too. There was nothing pretty about that Alston. He was mean and hard.

But that wasn't the worst. There were two big bundles, and those Alston insisted on taking along with us. I had to take one of them over my shoulder, and he took the other and waddled along with it, keeping one arm free for old Daggett. You can imagine that we couldn't make any particular good time, being bothered and loaded down like this. And now, behind us and above us, we heard a yell of surprise and rage.

The wagon had been stopped, and it was known that we weren't in it. Of course that was the meaning, and there was a secondary meaning that interested us a good deal. By the volume of that roar we knew that there must be at least five or six in the party, and now they would scatter and try to find us.

Well, with five of us making tracks through the woods, how could they help but make a quick find and then come boiling up around us? I said that to Alston, and he nodded and gritted his teeth as he looked back over his shoulder.

"That's like that hound Grenville," he snarled.

"He knew just when the best time would be for hitting. We should have waited for night before we started to come into the valley."

"We would have been smashed up in no time," I told him, "if we tried to cover this road by night. Besides, we're not beaten yet, but I think we'll have to fight before we're out of it. Is this why Grenville has been holding off? He's had men enough to eat up the party in the house."

"Of course!" snapped Alston. "What good would it have done him to grab the people at the house until this was there, too." And he jerked his head toward poor old Daggett who was tottering along between us.

Finally we managed to cover a mile and a half, I should guess, and there was no sound of any pursuit behind us. I knew that we would hear them a long time before we could see them. They would be sure to come on horses, and no horse in the world could wind his way silently through such a growth of brush and young saplings as grew through those woods.

We climbed up over the white ridge, where the big stones shoved their knees out of the ground. And then we could look straight ahead through the trees and see in the distance the form of the Daggett house, standing on the hill. It had a great effect on old Daggett. He threw out his arms toward it, and then he staggered out and away from Alston and me.

"Let him go," Alston said, frowning and watching very close. "He's got to get this out of his system some time."

"Ah, that is the place!" That was all Daggett would say, over and over: "Ah, that is the place!" Not a happy tone, like a man seeing an old friend, but a wild, desperate sort of a voice.

"He remembers," Alston said. "The old goat remembers more than I suspected."

We took hold of Daggett, one on either side of him. He gave us a wild look when we came up to him and grabbed him, and he made a faint struggle in our arms.

"Gentlemen," he said, "you have come for me, I see."

"We've come for you," Alston confirmed.

"Ah, well, I did not think it would be so soon," said Daggett, "but there is truth in the saying that blood cries up from the ground, and that murder will out. Murder will out, no matter if it be buried seven leagues under the ground."

He said it with a real agony in his throat, and I felt a wave of wonder and of fear. Because it didn't seem possible that this old fellow could ever have taken the life of another man.

"However," Daggett said, "I confess everything. There will be no need of a cross-questioning. And one of these trees will be quite as good as a scaffold for the hanging of my wretched body.

But, ah, may God forgive me. In my own house. In my own house!"

I looked at Alston. He was grinning with a sort of cold enjoyment, though the rest of us were all pretty sick. And I was almost glad when, right behind us, we heard horses smashing through the brush.

XIII

Well, as I was saying, that noise of the horses told us that trouble was coming and coming pretty fast. It broke up the concern with which we were watching poor old Daggett and listening to that talk of his that seemed to confess that he had been a murderer. With Grenville and his men smashing up behind us, I hardly knew what to think.

Alston said: "We got to put in among these rocks and try to stand them off."

He panted and pointed to a circle of rocks among the trees. But I could see in a minute the weakness of any scheme like that. The rock was all very well for gents on our own level. But what if Grenville and his tribe chose to slip up into the trees and fire down at us? They could butcher the lot of us as easy as if they had us herded into a pen.

But just what could be done looked hard to me to find out, when Lou came up beside me and lifted the bundle from my shoulder, where I was carrying it.

She jerked her head back. "You'll have to shoo them off, Doc," she said.

"Look here, Lou," I said, "are they a lot of flies, maybe, or deer, do you think?"

She just looked at me, and I knew my medicine, and I took it. I dropped back among the trees with old William Daggett making a terrible scene with Alston. He swore that he would die of shame if anybody but him turned back to face the danger. But they swung on through the trees and I saw no more of them while I looked back to see what sort of trouble would come my way.

Well, it came from two quarters. The gang of Grenville had been split into two sections. And those sections were driving up at us, one on either side of our trail.

The sun was down. I looked up between the great red trunks of the trees at the fire in the sky and the pure, deep blue of it up higher. There was a soft light everywhere, getting dimmer and dimmer, but it was enough light for shooting, and straight shooting, at that.

There were two things that might happen. I might turn loose some lead at the first riders I saw and turn them back, and that would give me a chance to slip away. Or else, when I started shooting, they might come right straight in. That would be the finish of me.

I got to a place not behind one of those whopping big trunks, but in a patch of brush in the center of an open space. From that spot I could see all around me pretty well, and there was enough brush to give me a sort of a screen, especially from men that were snap-shooting from the backs of horses.

I cuddled the butt of my rifle into the hollow of my shoulder and waited. And in another minute I heard horses crashing through the woods to the south of me—not far away, but just comfortably out of sight. I didn't like that. It meant that if I tackled the other lot, this southern mob would swing in and take me from the rear and scoop me up as easy as you please.

But straight before me came the other mischief. I heard someone shouting. I couldn't make out what, because the horses were making so much noise. Then three riders came in a bunch through the trees, with another pair behind them.

Of course by that time I was beginning to wish that I could make back tracks, but it was too late. A lot too late, even if I wanted to lie still, because all five of them were driving straight at the spot where I was lying in the shrubbery.

Well, I began to pull the trigger of that repeater faster than I ever pulled a trigger before in my life. I got a line just above their heads, and I fired three shots before they seemed to realize what was happening. Then I fired three more while they made for the trees, all yelling: "They're yonder in the brush! Scatter, boys!"

They got out of sight with a whoop, I can tell you, and I almost laughed. But I had no time to spend on laughing. My idea was to get their attention, and then, when they thought they had me at bay, to slip out on the far side of the shrubbery and so leave them there holding the bag, as you might say, with nothing at all in it.

But I needed speed if I was to succeed with that scheme. For I could hear the riders to the south of us shouting and coming on the wing to find out what was causing all the trouble. And all around me the trees were ringing with shouts and with the hoof strokes of the horses on rocks or through crackling brush as they tried to surround me.

I traveled like a snake and a little faster than most snakes, I think, until I got to the edge of the brush and saw before me, not more than six steps to the line of the woods, a flock of strong young saplings growing side by side like so many soldiers standing in a row.

But just as I raised up out of the brush, a rider came out of the trees from the south and with his revolver he put a pair of bullets not more than an inch past my nose. The smell of that lead, I might say, was all I wanted in the way of an argument to convince me that I should get back to the brush as fast as possible.

There were two other riders behind the first man, and one of the two was that same Henry Grenville. They all had their guns out and they threw a pound or two of lead to comb the bushes where I was. One of the slugs stung my leg. But there wasn't time to see what that wound was.

Those three crazy men were driving right at me as though they wanted to ride on top of me, and I had to send a couple of bullets whirring that way before I could check them and send them piling back for the shelter of the trees.

Well, I had them at a distance from me, now. But here they were in a circle around me. And by the way they whooped and carried on, you would have thought they had their hands filled with a treasure. However, it was a bad mess. If they wanted to see me in the open, all they had to do was to touch a match to that brush and let the flames do the rest.

I waited to hear what would happen, and yet I got a small sort of satisfaction from the knowledge that the rest of the party was skinning along through the woods and making fast tracks for the house of Daggett on the hill. They might very well be where I was now, if I hadn't chosen to come back here and turn this trick.

Then it jumped into my mind with a stab of pain that the girl had sent me here. It hadn't been my own idea at all. It had been Lou's hunch. And how could I tell what had made her suggest it? Well, when I had taken that thought home in me, like a bullet, it made me postpone looking at the wound in my leg again. Because the hurt in my heart was a lot greater.

Maybe you have guessed how far the pretty face, and the queer, careless way, and the strange eyes, and the husky voice of Lou had carried her with me. Well, I was wild about her. I had known her hardly an hour, and I was already lovesick for the first time.

It was the lowest time in my life, when I began to doubt Lou and her motives. I looked down at my leg, finally, and it wasn't much consolation to me to see that the bullet had only sliced along the surface of the flesh, just above the knee.

In the meantime a voice began calling: "Alston! Hello, Alston!"

It was the voice of Grenville. If he knew that Alston had been in the party, it showed that he was no fool. He had been taking it easy in the valley, waiting for Alston and his party to come. But from now on, Grenville would cut loose and do business. And things wouldn't be so very easy for the folks up there in the big house—not when they tried to get clear of Daggett Valley. No, that would be the time when they would wish they hadn't thrown me and my guns away.

XIV

I waited for another minute until Grenville called again: "It's no use, Alston! We know we've got you. You might as well talk turkey to me now as later."

Then I sang out: "Hello, Grenville! Doc Willis, speaking."

"Hello, Willis!" he answered me. "I hear you, but you're not the person I want to talk to just now. Tell Alston that he had better talk for himself."

Another idea came popping into my head. By this time there had been plenty of minutes for Alston and the girl and Grenville and Lou to get on to the Daggett house. But if I could show Grenville that they were not with me, he and the rest of his men might pile away on the trail, hoping to catch up with the others. And then that would leave me free to break out. Or, if only a part of them went, there would be less trouble for me to deal with the ones that were left.

So I said: "Grenville, it's no good. You'll never talk to Alston here."

"He's deaf and cursing the world, I suppose," laughed Henry Grenville, "but that makes no difference to me. I could burn out the pack of you, if it weren't that you have the girl with you."

"You know that, too?" I said.

"Yes, I know about everything, Alston."

"There's one thing you don't know," I said. "And that is that Alston and Daggett and the girl are not here now."

"Not there now?"

"I came back here to hold you fellows for a while, and I think I've done it long enough, Grenville."

The minute I named the idea, they seemed to see the point of it. There was a general shout of rage and disappointment, and I could hear them making for their horses again.

Grenville began to shout: "Stay where you are! Stay where you are, everybody! We've missed the rest of them by this time. Do you think that Doc Willis would show the cards before their game was won? But I tell you it's not won for them, by a long shot, if we can get Willis into our hands! Let us land Willis, and we'll have the others pretty much when we please!"

That sounded very like sense to me. In the whole crowd, Zack and Roger Beckett were not much use at fighting. That left Alston and Buck Logan to bear the brunt of the attack, and I didn't think they would have any very great luck in managing to hold off Grenville and his men.

However, here was Grenville sending his fellows back to their posts. The shadows were gathering pretty thick and fast.

He called: "Well, are you ready to come out, Willis?"

"What sort of a deal will you make with me?" I answered him.

He replied in a way that nearly took my breath. "You come with us, and I'll make you pretty good terms!"

Generous? Why, it was almost foolish. Here I was out of the picture, and all he had to do was to wait for his time to put a chunk of lead through me. But instead of that, he offered to take me on his crew as though I was a free man and had never done him a stroke of harm.

I said: "Will you let me come and talk with you on that?"

"Come out as free as you please," said Grenville.

"Show yourself first," I said. "Some of your gents ain't very friendly to me, and they might use the chance to shoot from behind."

"Here I am," Grenville said, and he stepped out into the open, as brave as ever he was. There was nothing of the yellow streak in that Grenville.

So I got up, in my turn, and walked out of the brush. I said: "I've come out here to talk to you, Grenville, because you're terribly white, it seems to me. But the first thing I've got to say to you is that I can't go to work for you. I can't switch horses in the middle of the stream."

"Is that final?"

"It is," I said.

"Well," said Grenville, "just tell me, if you please, what you expect me to do with you?"

"You're the boss," I said. "I'd suggest something like this. They've got your brother. And you've got me. See if they won't arrange a trade for him?"

"They have Larry?" Grenville cried.

"Why, man, didn't you know that?"

He only groaned: "Is it true, Willis?"

"It's true."

"If they do him a harm," said Grenville, "I'll flay them alive." Looking pretty sick and weak, he added: "I never should have let him come. Think of a lad like that, blasting a fine life, with a sordid adventure . . ." He broke off and snapped at me: "What happened?"

"About Larry?"

"Yes."

"He took a pot shot at me this morning, and my horse, Jupe, got his head between the rifle and me. Jupe died, and I hit the ground alive. Afterward I got up behind Larry. Him and me had a little mix. And I persuaded him to come along with me, real friendly."

"Damn it, Willis," he said. "You were born to ruin my plans. Is the boy hurt?"

"Not a scratch."

"And yet you had him under after he'd killed your horse?"

"That was it."

He rubbed his hard knuckles across his chin and stared at me. "All right, Doc," he said. "I'd like to turn you loose and let you go on your way for this, but before I can do that, I've got to try my hand at getting my brother loose from Alston . . . and Buck Logan."

He hesitated a little before he used that name, which made me suspect that he thought the opposition to the scheme would come from Buck alone.

"You persuade Alston," I said, "and I'll swear that Buck will do what he can to get me back."

"Do you think so?" Grenville smiled. "Well, son, let me tell you this . . . they know that while they have my brother, they have a weapon that will keep me from bothering them a mite. If they can get the stuff they're after, they can walk right out of the valley with it, and I'll never be able to raise a hand at them, because they know that Larry means a lot more to me than all the money in the world. You understand? Now, Doc, you've had a chance to size up both Buck and Alston. Tell me frankly, do you really think that either of them would prefer your safety to a fair chance to get away with the loot?"

I thought it over, and a lot of black thoughts swarmed up into my mind.

"About Alston I know," I said. "He'd never

turn his hand to do me a good turn, or anybody else, except one."

"Meaning the girl," said Grenville.

"You seem pretty well informed," I couldn't help saying to him.

"Why, Willis," he said, "I know enough about that crew to be sick of them. But I could tell Alston, if I had the chance, that the girl is not for him. She has too much sense. He thinks he can buy her, but he can't . . . not in one short life."

That pleased me a good deal. "What do you know about her?" I asked.

He squinted at me, and then smiled. "Has she hit you, too?" Grenville asked. "Well, she has a way about her, I admit. No doubt about that. But she's made quick work with you. Well, I know enough about her to respect her, if that's what you mean. But what you say about Buck Logan interests me a lot. Do you really think that he would put a high value on you, old-timer?"

"Do you think I'm wrong?" I said.

"You can see that I think that. But we'll see who's right in the long run. We'll not have far to run, at that. We'll go up there to the house and propose a dicker. A trade of you for my brother, and if Logan is the white man you think he is, he'll certainly see that the trade is made, rather than leave you in our hands. Isn't that right?"

I admitted that it was.

And so, in another five minutes I found myself sitting behind Grenville on his horse. He hadn't asked me to give my word that I wouldn't try to escape on the way. He didn't have to, because the rest of his gang were riding along behind us, and I would as soon have jumped into the fire as tried to get away under the guns of that lot. I studied them in the evening light, and I'll tell you they were a hardy lot.

"Where did you get these thugs?" I asked Grenville.

"The finest lot of cut-throats out of jail," he chuckled, "but they'll serve their purpose. Here we are, old-timer. Now we'll see what happens with your friend in the Daggett house."

XV

We came upon the house from behind one of the nearest trees in the edge of the clearing that surrounded the old place. Grenville started shouting. and, in a few seconds, a window was thrown up by someone who took care to keep out of sight of us.

The voice of Buck Logan called out: "Hello, Grenville!"

Henry Grenville answered: "I've come to talk business."

"Old son," said Buck, and his voice was that of a gent who is pretty well pleased with himself, "tell me what you got to say."

"I've come to show you how generous I can be," Grenville said. "If you wish to listen."

"Fire away."

"I have some property that belongs to your side of the fence," Grenville said.

"Have you?"

"You can guess what that property is."

"You mean Doc Willis, I suppose?"

"That's what I mean."

Buck Logan laughed, and, as the big sound of his laughter came floating out to me, it made me wince, I can tell you.

Grenville looked aside at me. "How does that sound to you?" he asked.

"Wait a minute," I said. "The party ain't over yet. We'll do the voting at the end of it."

"Just as you say. Listen."

There was the big throat of Buck Logan bellowing: "I hear what you have to say, Grenville! I never thought much of you as a businessman, but I do now. You want to drive a bargain, do you?"

"That's what I'm here for."

"And you know that we have something that belongs to you, too? You know that, Grenville?"

"You have," Grenville admitted.

"Do you aim to say that the two parties should be exchanged?"

"Why not?" said Grenville. "That kid brother of mine is no hand with a gun, and Willis is your fighting ace."

"You've told one lie," I said in an undertone. "That brother of yours shoots straight enough to satisfy me."

"I like the way you talk up," Buck said, "but I've got to say that you're looking at this thing pretty crooked, old-timer. I'd like nothing better than to make a friendly deal with you, but you got to look at it this way . . . so long as I have your brother, I've got you in my pocket. I'll have no trouble with you so long as I have him." And he broke out with his laughter again.

It brought a growl from Grenville. "Willis is thanking you for what you have to say," he cut in.

I could hear Buck Logan suddenly begin to swear in a deep rumble. "Is Willis there with you?" he asked.

"Willis is here," said Grenville.

"Hello, Doc!" called Logan.

"Hello," I responded, pretty feeble.

"Are you well, old man?"

"I'm well enough," I said.

"Mind you," said Buck, "Grenville is a white man . . . and I know that you're in no danger with him. Otherwise, I'd cut off an arm to have you clean away from him."

I didn't make any answer. It was pretty thin talk, after what I had stood there and heard him saying just before.

"You there still, Doc?" called Buck, pretty anxious.

"Oh, I'm here," I said. "And I'm listening. Have you got any more to say?"

"Lots more!" Buck Logan called. "And in the first place . . ."

"We've heard enough," said Grenville. "I brought Doc here mostly to let him see what a hound you are, Logan, and, if I am not mistaken, I'll have him lined up against you before the morning!"

"Line him up!" shouted Logan. "Line up a

hundred more like him. Welcome to them, old-timer. But what I want you to notice is that I'll still have your brother Larry along with me, and while I have him, I'm not worrying, Grenville." He broke off, laughing again.

Grenville swore softly, under his breath. He called out: "I'm going off, Logan, but I expect you'll come to your senses after a time! You may think that I put a higher value on my brother than the case is, but you may be wrong . . . never forget that. And if you're wrong, with Doc Willis on my side, I can eat the rest of you alive, Logan! You hear me?"

"Good!" said Logan. "It'd be a fine meal. Especially considering what we'll have in our pockets before long. So long, old-timer! Keep a watch on this house, and, if I change my mind, I'll show you a pair of lights in this window."

"I hear you!" Grenville shouted. "So long!"

He talked cool enough, but he was pretty sick at this sort of talk, and, as he went back through the trees, he hardly had the energy to tell a couple of his men to keep a watch over the house.

As he walked on with me, he said: "You've heard, Doc?"

"I heard," I admitted.

"And what do you think?"

"I'm not thinking," I said.

"Come," he said. "You have to confess that I was a good prophet. I told you what would happen, and what I said has turned out to be true. Is that right?"

I admitted that it was right, and I had to admit it with a groan. "I treated him white, Grenville," I explained, to let him know why I was so badly cut up.

"Of course you did . . . and you treat most people white, perhaps too white for your own good. If you had aimed to kill when we came up with you back there in the wood, perhaps you would be inside that house, yonder, and we would be burying our dead back in the clearing. However, let that go. I have two things to say. The first is the least important. It is that I still want you with me, and that I'll pay you five thousand dollars. The second is that I like you, my friend, and, if you play with me, you'll have a chance to see all of the cards laid upon the table, face up."

"Right," I said. "I like what you say fine. And I dunno what it is that holds me back. It ain't that I care what people will say about me. I've had myself damned in about every known way, a long time before this. But, as a matter of fact, I don't think that I can go in with you, Grenville."

"You're sure?"

"I suppose I am."

"Will you give me one good reason?"

"I'll try to."

"You can't doubt that those fellows in there are all thugs."

"Daggett?" I said.

"Daggett?" he said, and his face and his voice softened a lot. "That poor old man. I'm sorry to know that he's in their hands, because he'll get no good out of it, whatever they may find in the house."

"No good at all?"

"From those stone-hearted devils? I should say not!"

I shook my head. It was pretty hard talk, but I was beginning to feel that Grenville was as right as the fellows in that house were wrong.

He went on: "What I want you to see for yourself is that, if they will treat you badly now, they would plan to treat you badly even if you were with them, working heart and soul for them. Doesn't that stand to reason?"

I had to admit that there was a good deal in what he had to say, and he added: "Oh, I know them and I hate them as much as you'll come to hate them before you're done with them." Then he made a pause, finally saying: "Give me your answer, Doc."

I said: "I'd like to do it, but I started in this game with Logan and his crew inside of that house. They've never cut me off of their list. And I've got no more from them and this game than I might have expected from anybody that I was working for . . . unless he was my friend. And I think that I'll have to stick by them, Grenville."

"Ah, well," he said, "I'll change your mind for you before the morning. I've got to. Because if they have Larry, I've got to have something on my side of the fence to play off against that power . . . and what can it be except you? What can it be?"

Just then there was a call from the trees toward the house: "Hey, chief, they've started in showing two lights from that window . . . !"

I could hardly believe it, and Grenville shouted with his surprise, but when we ran back through the woods and came to the spot, we saw that he had told us right. There were two lights burning from the window where Logan said he would show them if he decided he must change this mind.

And they looked mighty good to me, I can tell you.

XVI

Grenville seemed hardly able to believe his eyes. And he kept saying over and over: "I can't make it out. For Logan or Alston to do a thing like this . . . I can't make it out."

Well, for my part, I thought that when they had had a chance to consider everything, they had decided that it would be better not to leave me in the lurch, and so they had changed their minds.

There wasn't much of a dicker. Grenville just called out to make out what the meaning of the two lights in the window might be, and the answer came right back that it was what I wished for—Larry Grenville was to be turned over for me in a fair exchange. Out came Larry Grenville, walking straight down the path of the lamplight and into the same path I walked freely toward the house. We met in the center, and Larry held out his hand.

"I thought I was done for in that fine gang of thugs, old-timer. I'm glad you were out there to make the exchange, but will you tell me one thing?"

"I'd like to if I can, Larry."

"How the devil did you ever hook up with such a low crowd?"

He didn't mean to be sassy. He was just

speaking his mind out—and that was no great compliment to Alston, big Buck Logan, and the rest.

"They may look low to you," I told him, "and they may be low, but they're the crowd that I'm playing this game with, and they'll have to do for me." I could not help adding: "This here business is apt to turn into a fight before long. And I give you one word of advice, keep clear of me, Larry, because you've used up your share of luck with me. But tell me one thing, what made them change their minds about making the exchange?"

"Can't you guess, you lucky dog?" asked Larry Grenville. "Why, it was the girl, of course. She just put down her foot and said she wouldn't take a step in the direction they wanted her to go until she saw you back in the house."

Take it all in all, I think that was about the best news I had ever heard.

"Thanks, Larry," I said. "I sure appreciate you telling me this."

He grinned at me in rather a crooked fashion. "It's all right, Doc," he said. "I was a loser with her before I ever had a chance to be a winner. So long."

He held out his hand. I took it with a good, hard grip, and then he passed on toward the woods, and I went on toward the Daggett house.

When I got to the door, there was Alston, opening it for me, and giving me a sort of a dark, sour, upward glance. He met me in silence, and I passed him and went on into the house, hating him with all my heart, I can tell you. Right back there in the hall I met Buck, and there was a good deal of difference. He came straight up to me and stretched out his big bear paw of a hand.

"Why, old-timer," he said, "damn me if it ain't good to see you back here with us."

I looked Buck straight in the eye and tried to read something behind his big, ugly face. But all I could see there seemed like honesty, to me. Every time I came near him, lately, he had seemed more and more like a puzzle to me. I said: "Look here, Buck. I stood out yonder under the trees, and listened to the talk you made with Grenville. What was I to make of that?"

"What were you to make of it?" Buck said. "Why, simply this . . . that I know Henry Grenville is a white man, and that you were in no danger with him."

"That sounds reasonable, Buck," I said, "but the fact is that while I was listening to you, it seemed to me that you didn't give a damn whether you would ever see me again. But beyond all that is the fact that while Grenville is a white man, right enough, he has a lot of thugs with him that hate my heart and that would plant me full of lead, if they had more than half a chance."

"Don't tell me that, Doc," Buck insisted. "Don't tell me that, old boy."

"You didn't know it?"

"Know it? Of course not!"

I stared at him, trying to make out whether he was joking, or whether he was really in earnest. He seemed in earnest, and there was nothing I could do to get at the real truth in him. If he wanted to deceive me, there was no doubt that he could do it. I was no match for that smooth-talking way that he had with him. He was altogether too deep for me.

I asked after Daggett, then, and Buck told me that Daggett had been in a terrible state by the time they got him to the house, and that he had been so nervous and cut up that they had put him to bed and quieted him down with an opium pill that Alston had.

"Old Daggett is pretty far spent," said Buck, "but he knew his house. He's pretty far gone, but, still, he knew his house. And that was one thing. However, I don't think he'll stay long in this here house. Not very long. And not long in this life, either, Doc, if I'm not mistaken."

I agreed with that. Because anybody with half an eye could see that the poor old fellow was about two thirds dead. Then I asked if I could see Lou Wilson.

Buck dropped his head a little and frowned, very thoughtful.

I snapped out: "Tell me straight. Are you afraid for me to see the girl?"

"No, I'm not afraid," he said.

But no matter what his words were, I knew that he meant something different. He was afraid. He was mighty afraid. Well, I could see him thinking the thing over, pretty careful, and then he said: "Go ahead. You see Lou and talk with her. Only . . . you won't try to mix into her business and ours too much?" He looked at me with a frown, and I could see that he was on the edge of saying something more. But he checked himself and he only remarked: "Well, you go ahead and see her. She's upstairs. The first room on the right."

So I went up the stairs, thinking things over slowly and, when I got to the first room on the right, I tapped at the door.

"Come in!" sang out the voice of Lou.

I opened the door and went in. And there was Lou standing in front of a mirror with her fine hair streaming down her back—but that hair that had been a fine brown during the day, was a bright, shining red at night.

XVII

I don't mean that that was the only change. Her face was changed, too. There was a deep blue look about the eyes that had been gray in the daytime—gray and sky-blue, if you know what I mean. But here at night there was nothing about them except the deep violet blue that the eyes of beautiful women sometimes have.

I had never noticed her eyelashes before in the daytime, but now, though it was only the night, I could see them perfectly clear and fine, and that was a great surprise to me. They were jet black, and long.

But that wasn't all. No, even her skin had changed. It had been a fine, healthy-looking sort of a brownish skin before—an olive skin, if anything. But now it was very different, it was all pink and white. It was the sort of a skin that an eleven-year-old girl has before the sun has begun to roughen her up, and change her a lot, and make her wrinkled around the eyes. No, sir, she was so different that you wouldn't believe it, and that neck and throat of hers, that had been almost as brown as an Indian's, was now as snowy and polished-up looking as a queen's might have been. I was a good deal surprised, of course, and I hung there in the doorway and stared like a fool.

"Confound it," Lou said, and stamped on the floor. "Confound it, how was I to remember that you were back in the crowd again."

I could see that she would not have cared if any of the others had popped in to see her, but I was different. I didn't know whether to be flattered or just sad. I said: "Look here, Lou, what's wrong with you and your hair? Or are you Lou Wilson?"

"I'm her twin sister," Lou said sarcastically. "I'm the red-haired, blue-eyed kid, and don't you forget it."

Well, it was her voice. She might change the rest of herself, complete as a picture painted over, but she couldn't change that husky voice. It was Lou, right enough.

"What's happened?" I asked.

"I tumbled in a stack of paints," Lou replied, "that's all. Does it bother you a lot, old-timer?"

I couldn't speak for a minute.

"Do I look like the devil?" Lou asked.

"Nearly," I said.

She took up a mirror and squinted at herself. "Why," she said, "the way it looks to me, I'm very nearly beautiful, in this rig."

"Lou, you take it from me. You was never meant to be beautiful."

She dropped the mirror and swung around at me. "Say, Doc, how do you get that way?" she snapped. "Am I as homely as all that?"

"I don't mean homely," I said, "but the fact is, Lou, that you . . ."

"Never mind," she interrupted. "Don't explain. When I want to get the truth, I'll come to you. When I want to be happy, I'll go to somebody else."

Well, that was a good deal of a settler for me, as you can see for yourself, but at the same time, I wasn't finished. "What's it all going to be about?" I asked her.

But just then a pair of voices floated up toward us through the open window and Lou didn't answer.

It was old man Daggett, and Buck Logan was there walking along with him.

We heard Daggett say: "In the morning I shall take you for a ride up and down the valley, as far as we can go."

"The whole length of it, Mister Daggett?" Buck said, very respectful. "Will we have time for that in one day?"

Daggett laughed a little. "You wouldn't think there was time, my friend Logan, looking at those trees. But let me tell you that the good road by which you came into the valley is continued up and down the entire length of it. I had it cut out . . . and I built little bridges over every creek and gully, so that one can ride at a hot pace through the entire length and breadth of Daggett Valley . . ." He stopped but added quickly:

"Excuse me for giving it that name. But about a year ago, you understand, some of the miners who had struck it rich here began to call the valley after my name . . . and it's become rather a habit here."

That took my breath, but I could see what had happened. Poor old Daggett had been snatched back to the old days, that long, long time ago, when Daggett Valley was still packed with miners, and when he had been the king of the place, looked up to, and worshiped, and respected a lot by everybody. Yes, he was back in those old days, and he was taking Buck Logan around and treating him like a guest and trying to make him happy.

Somehow that gave me a sort of a tear in the eye, to hear Daggett talk like that. You could see in a flash just what sort of a fellow he had been in those old days, mighty generous, trying to make other folks happy, free and easy, proud of his fortune, and wanting to show it off to other folks.

"It'll be a fine trip," Buck Logan said. "It'll be fine to go with you, Mister Daggett."

"It will be my privilege," said the old man, and then he stopped. For he had caught the sound of Lou's voice, she having exclaimed something about old man Daggett reliving the past.

"No," old Daggett said. "That was not my wife. Her voice is pitched high, and very light. It must be one of the servants."

"I been sort of wondering," Buck Logan said, "how Missus Daggett would get on out here in the wilderness, as you might call it."

"Ah," old Daggett said. "Do you think it will be hard for a lady to be happy out here?"

"No, no," answered Buck. "That wasn't what I meant to say. Sure she could be happy here. Look at a fine, big house like this . . . why, any woman would be pretty proud and glad to live in it, I should say."

"I think so, too," Daggett said, pretty self-satisfied. "I think so, too. Why couldn't she be happy here? A little restless at first, perhaps. But soon the beauty of the forest would begin to work on her mind . . ." He was getting pretty excited.

"There ain't any doubt that you're right," said Buck Logan. "Besides," he added in a sort of a leading voice, "sometimes it's a good thing to get folks away from the city . . . a lot of bad things in the cities, bad for the men and bad for the women."

He said that with just a little weight on the last word, and I wondered that he dared to, but Daggett broke out with a groan: "Ah, Logan, that is true. That is bitterly true, of course. But here in the wilderness, a man can forget his past. And a woman can forget hers. Is not that true?"

"Nothing truer was ever said," remarked Buck Logan.

Well, that was enough explanation for the crazy

thing that old Daggett had done in building this house away out here in the wilderness. It was something about his wife—no freak of his own, but a thing that he had done for her sake. And I couldn't help pitying him more than ever, for he seemed almost tragic.

But I couldn't fit everything together. I couldn't make out the murder that he accused himself of. There were a thousand blanks in the true story that lived around the memory of the Daggett house. And, as I stood there in the night, I wondered how long it would be before I got at the truth. Or if I ever would? I was a lot closer to the time than I guessed. And before the morning came I was to know everything that could be told of Daggett, and his poor wife, and Alston—yes, and of Carberry, too.

Well, just then the voice of Alston sang out: "Hello, Buck, are you there?"

"Here I am," Buck answered.

"It's about time," Alston said.

"All right," Buck said.

"By heaven," gasped Daggett, "whose voice is that?"

"Why do you ask?" Buck asked.

"Because it sounded to me . . . no, it can't be . . . but it sounded to me like the voice of that archdevil, Alston."

XVIII

What a chill it sent through me to hear that. There was a man and a voice that Daggett had been traveling with for days and days, and suddenly he recognized it like a flash. But I suppose that being brought back to the old place had cleared up his brain. Not all of it, perhaps—he was still a long distance from the normal. But he had recovered enough to have bright spots as well as the darkness. So it was that he recognized the voice of Alston—not out of the present, but out of the past of those long years ago.

There was electricity in the air, I can tell you. Right then I had the sense of a tragedy that was to come.

Buck took Daggett back into the house, and, as I watched him go, I wondered if the old man wasn't like a bull taken to the slaughter. I wondered if he'd ever come out again, alive.

After a minute, out came Buck, and I heard his voice calling softly: "Doc. Oh, Doc Willis."

I looked at Lou, and she nodded her head for me to go. I sneaked out, and then I waited until he called again. After that, I answered him, and I went out, because I didn't want him to think that maybe I had been overhearing what had been said between him and Daggett.

"You're here, eh?" said Buck.

"Yes."

"Have you seen old Daggett lately?"

"No," I said. "Is he missing?"

"Not missing," Buck answered, "but I wondered . . . well, let it go."

Of course he was hinting that perhaps I had overheard the conversation, but he thought that perhaps it wasn't important enough to emphasize.

He said: "There hasn't been a sound from the woods, eh?"

"No," I told him, "there hasn't."

"Seems strange," Buck Logan said, "that Grenville should lie out there so quiet, in spite of all the men he has with him. Don't it seem strange to you?"

"Yes," I admitted, "it sure does."

"What do you think he could have up his sleeve?"

"No idea in the world."

"He's planning some sort of trouble . . . some sort of real trouble for us," Buck assured me, "you can depend on that. He isn't the sort of fellow who would waste his time."

"I suppose not," I said.

"But you're keeping watch for us?" Buck said, quick and sharp.

"Am I the only one to keep up that job?" I asked.

"Not the only one, of course," said Buck.

"We're all keeping an eye peeled. But Zack and Roger Beckett, they ain't of much use, as you know . . . and me and Alston have Daggett on our hands."

"Sure," I said. "Is there anything special up tonight?"

"Special? Tonight?" Buck said, and cleared his throat. "No, not tonight. The only reason I came out here was to tell you that we appreciate you, Doc. Also, I wanted to ask you to keep a sharp look-out now that we have the girl and Daggett here along with us."

"Sure," I said. "I understand. This here Grenville has been holding back and taking things easy, hoping that, when the time comes, he would be able to scoop up Daggett and the girl, either coming into the valley or after they got here. Ain't that right?"

"Exactly, Doc. Exactly."

"And now that the two of them are here, Grenville is going to cut loose pretty soon."

"Yes," said Buck, "and you never can tell when. A slippery devil, that chap Grenville is. Got a brain in his head that's working all the time, and you won't forget it."

"I won't forget it," I told Buck.

"And you'll stay busy on the job?"

"I will."

"I'll shake with you on that," said Buck.

Well, I took his hand in the dark, and then he

started back toward the house. He strolled along, and he even whistled a note or two of a song, and then he went inside. By that time I was standing on a needle's edge, for I was beginning to expect things to happen. There were a lot of reasons for what I expected to happen.

In the first place, there was no occasion why Buck should've made a point of looking me up there in the night except for a very definite purpose. And that was that he might want to make sure that he had got me outside of the house—important because of something that he and Alston wanted to do inside of it.

So I made up my mind to a number of things. I decided that right on this first night Alston and Logan were going to try to make their big play. And I decided, in addition to that, that they were going to try to make it right away. But what was I to do? I couldn't guess what they would be about. I knew that it must have something to do with the make-up that the girl was wearing, but just what Lou was to be used for beat me complete.

Well, I looked over the house and I could see several windows lit. One was the dining room. And one was the room of old man Daggett, to the front of the house. I turned the corner of the place, and saw another lit window, one that opened out onto a little balcony, built strong and snug against the side of the house.

I decided right there that I would have to take

a look, because I had to do something, and, guessing as much as I guessed, I would have gone plumb mad if I had had to stand around and look at the stars when robbery—murder—I didn't know what all—might be taking place in the Daggett house.

The side of the house was pretty easy to climb on account of the big supports of the balcony that come down right to the ground. I climbed up, taking care not to make any sound at all, and I honestly think that nobody standing right under me could've heard a whisper from my work.

A good thing that I was so silent, too, because when I got to the outer edge of the balcony and lifted up, I saw that a man had reached the balcony ahead of me. However, the important thing was not what was outside the window. It was what was inside the window. And that was about the queerest picture I had ever seen before—queerer, I'd make a guess, than you have ever seen, either.

There was a table right in the center of the space that I looked into through the window, and up to this table there were two chairs drawn. And in one chair sat Lou, but fixed up so you would never know her. Of course you can guess that she was made up the way I had seen her not a little while before, but that wasn't all. Her face was changed, then, but her clothes were changed now. She wore a big, broad, black hat, with a black feather curling down one side of it, and the brim looped up on the other side, like the pictures of riding hats you used to see in some of the old-fashioned books. And she had on a tailored suit, and around her neck there was a big brown fur, that looked like real fox, and mighty expensive. She had on a pair of black kid gloves, long and fancy-looking—I mean to say that she had one of those gloves on, but the other glove was off and held in the covered hand. And the hand that was bare, why, it shone like anything. So that you wouldn't believe it. On one of the fingers of it there was a diamond that sparkled and glittered something wonderful to see. Yes, she had used up a considerable deal of whiting on those brown hands of her.

On the far side of the table from her there was a gent that I didn't know, at first. He wore longish black hair, and he had straight black eyebrows that gave him sort of a devilish look. And he was smooth-shaven. He wore a black coat, padded out on the shoulders, the way coats used to be worn, a long time ago.

But in a minute this fellow smiled, and, by something in his smile, I knew him. Perhaps you've guessed already—yes, it was Alston. It was Alston, with his mean smile, but his gray beard was gone, which showed a good chin, and a straight, cruel, cunning mouth. He had covered up his gray hair with a longish black wig, with the hair of it brushed back a good deal, giving him a sort of an artistic look. And he wore a black silk cravat with a big diamond pin stuck into it—big enough and shining enough to stop a train with, I can tell you.

But I haven't told you all. I'll tell you that on the table between the two of them there was a smooth gray chamois bag, all crumpled up, and spilled out of the mouth of the bag, there was a whole double handful of jewels.

By this time my slow brain was beginning to translate what I was seeing into the facts of the case. I knew, now, that this was a real effort to reproduce something that had been in this same room a long time before. But what could that be?

Pretty soon, Alston says: "Hush, Lou. What was that?"

"Somebody walking up the stairs," she answered him.

"Aye," said Alston, after listening for a moment. "But is it time? No, not for ten minutes, according to what Carberry promised."

"Carberry?" gasped Lou, looking white even under her make-up.

"Why not Carberry?" Alston said. "He won't eat you."

"Carberry . . . the murderer," Lou hissed.

"Damn it," said Alston, "I suppose I shouldn't've used that name. But I tell you, you'll never see Carberry's face . . . no matter how deep he may be in this thing."

"Ah," Lou said, with a quick glance over her shoulder toward the window, "I feel as if somebody was sneaking up behind me with a knife in his hand. Carberry . . ."

She was hard hit, and no wonder, considering the reputation Carberry wore around those parts of the world.

"Get ready," said Alston. "Because I think they're surely coming."

"What'll I do?"

"Lean back in your chair and, with your ungloved hand, grab at the jewels. You see?"

"Jewels?" she said with a grin.

"Well, they look close enough to the real thing. I had this stuff made one at a time, to look like the real things . . . and I don't think I missed out, very far. He'll never know the difference unless he's seeing clearer than I think the poor old goat can do today. He's too upset to notice any of the details, I think. Lean back in your chair . . . so."

She leaned back and grabbed at the jewels with one hand, just as he had said, and then Alston said: "I've got to lean over you now and pretend to be kissing you. You understand, Lou?"

"Did his wife do that?" Lou asked.

"Why, she lost her head when she saw that there was a chance to get away from this place . . . worked out like a story. She spends all his money. Poor Daggett comes West to try to recoup. And he does, because he hits gold, with regular beginner's luck. After he's raked in a lot of the yellow stuff, he thinks that he'll bring his wife West and keep her safely here away from all temptation to run up big bills and flirt with the boys. A wild man's notion. She would have gone mad in this place. And if it hadn't been for that, she would never have looked at . . ." He stopped himself.

"Never have looked as low as a gambler?" Lou said.

"Confound your sharp tongue," Alston said. "No matter. The main thing was that he walked in and found us . . . Listen . . . they're coming toward this place."

"Yes, right up the stairs . . ."

"And now down the hall. Hold this position, Lou . . . you hear me?"

He took her in his arms and put his face close to hers, and I think he would have made it more than just a pretense if she hadn't said: "If you really kiss me, Al, I'll sink a knife in you. You hear me?"

"You spitfire. You little devil," he whispered through his teeth. "It would be almost worth it. Steady . . . don't tremble. That might give everything away. I'm the one who runs through the danger . . . not you."

"Very well," said Lou. "I won't throw the game away, now that we've played it this far."

"Hush."

I could hear the pair of feet stop outside the door—though they had been apparently trying to move very soft and easy. And in that minute I remember that my heart nearly stopped beating, and yet I had a chance to think of two things— the fierce, bright eyes of Lou, looking up to Alston, and the shadowy head of the gent outside the window.

Is that shadowy head Carberry? I wondered.

And then the door opened . . .

XIX

Outside the door stood Daggett, looking almost as small as a boy in comparison with the figure of the giant behind him. I thought that that shadow of a man behind must be Buck Logan, but just then he side-stepped back out of view, and I couldn't be sure. Daggett, I expected, would shout or make a start. But he didn't. He just walked into that room with a sort of a puzzled frown on his face, like a man who isn't quite sure of what he's seeing, and then he rubbed his knuckles across his forehead.

He leaned a hand against the wall. "Good God," Daggett said. "This is what I saw in my dream."

When he spoke, Alston jumped up and away, as though in surprise, and, as he jumped away, Lou leaned forward and covered her face with her hands, shuddering with real fear.

"Alston," said Daggett, "I knew I should find you here. Don't ask me how. God showed this thing to me, and I knew it must be."

"God or the devil," Alston declared. "Stand away from that door, Daggett, or I'll do you harm."

"Are you running away?" Daggett asked. "And are you leaving your woman behind you?"

Lou gave a twist and a sort of a moan. Alston

backed into a corner of the room, with his right hand always behind him and in his hip pocket. I never saw a man do any better acting.

"Daggett," he said, "you're wrong. She's not mine. Only . . . just now . . ."

"Just now you planned to run away with this? Is that all? And she is wearing a hat . . . by accident, I suppose?" He stepped to the side and looked at her. "And a riding skirt, too," he said.

"Curse it, man," said Alston, "I want to explain . . ."

"Hush," Daggett said very grandly. "Hush, Alston. Don't you suppose I understand perfectly? I understand everything. And the reason you wanted me to put more and more money into jewels, Martha, I understand that, too. There's only one thing that rather bothers me . . . not more than a third of those fine fellows are mine. And where did you get the others? Where did you get the others, Alston . . . or should I ask that question of you, my dear wife?"

You could see that he was holding himself back with a hand of iron, but all the time I kept waiting for that iron hand to snap.

Alston glared at Daggett, and then at Lou, but Lou did not stir. Daggett picked up a big ruby—a monster and a sparkler.

"Here's a beauty," he said, "that must have cost a good many tens of thousands. I know a bit about the prices of rubies, now, and I wonder

134

arnest. He brought his old gun down on t[
[and fired.

[ston let his Colt drop with a clatter to th
[, and he clasped his hands over his head an
[gered forward. He pitched on his face besid
[able and twisted over on his back and la[
[in a sprawling shape, with a great smear o[
[own his face and through his hair, and in hi[
[I could see the little red sponge with which
[done the trick—in or under his hand, away
[the view of Daggett.

[for Daggett, he stood up, stiff and straight
[minute, and then dropped the gun into his
[pocket.

[knew it would happen exactly like this,"
[id quietly. "I knew it with a very strange
[nowledge. Martha, God have pity on your
[hed soul, because you were the cause of
[You were the cause of this . . ."

[at once there was a heavy knocking at the
[of the house. It made my hair stand on
[and it seemed to throw a terrible chill into
[ett. He had been as calm as could be, up to
[oint, but now he went off the handle in a
[way, throwing his hands above his head. He
[d into a child, very pitiful to see.

[artha!" he yelled. "What shall I do? Oh,
[shall I do? Help me, Martha, in heaven's
[Help me, I pray you!"

[only flung herself out of her chair, without

138

how much this thing cost. More than a hundred thousand, I should say. A hundred thousand in one sparkler. Ah, Martha, you and Alston truly have high stakes on the table. Very high." He looked across at Alston and tried to smile, but it was a terrible poor excuse for a smile that he worked up.

"More of them, too," he said, "a great many more. Why, Martha, you've let yourself in for your share of a very tidy fortune, here. A great deal more than I could offer you at present it seems. A great deal more." His smooth voice warbled a bit, here, and his hand went up to his wrinkled old throat. He went on: "I see no good reason why I should not take these jewels and the rest, which belong to me, and try to ascertain if they may not have been stolen . . . as mine were about to be. Do you think of any good reason to advance against this, Alston?" And he scooped the stuff all together and raked it into the chamois bag.

"Will you look at me, Martha?" he said. "Poor girl, are you really going to give up everything and go off with a rascally gambler like Alston? Alston of all the men in the world. How will you be considered in the East, after this is known? You should know . . . because that world means a great deal more to you than it could ever mean to me."

He put the chamois bag into his pocket, and, as

135

he did that, Alston barked at him: "Daggett, drop that bag on the table, do you hear me? Put it back where you found it!"

"You speak harshly," Daggett said, looking more at Lou, believing she was his wife, than at Alston.

"I mean business," said Alston. "Your own stuff you may take out, but the rest has no concern of yours attached to it."

"How can I be sure of that?" Daggett asked gravely. "I tell you that the property of every honest man is the concern of every other honest man. And how can I tell that these sparklers really belong to you . . . and to Martha?"

"No other person has claimed them," Alston said.

"I claim them, then," said Daggett, "until the law decides otherwise."

"Daggett!" barked Alston, raising his voice sharp and hard.

"Don't do it," Daggett said, shaking his head in a sort of a sad fashion. "Don't bring out your gun, Alston. I warn you that this evening I am armed. And the truth of what will happen here is revealed to me . . . I cannot say by what marvelous foresight. But if you draw your weapon, I shall shoot you through the head and leave you dead on this floor . . . stretched beside the table, there. I have seen it all in a vision, Alston, and the very manner of your fall. I beg you in the name

of heaven, believe what I am tellir have planned too much harm against and you are given into my hands nc believe me, Alston?"

Alston, backed into the farthes the room, swayed a little from side it was wonderful to see the way h and shame and a pretended desi faked jewels fight in his face. Bu said: "Well, let it go. I only want y Daggett, that you are changing parts becoming the real robber where I w to be a robber. And what the lav you . . ."

"I shall be very willing to meet to face," Daggett said, "quite as v perhaps a little more so . . . thar But . . ." He broke off, then ac warned you, Alston. Beware of me!

"Curse you and your warnings, "And take this!"

He snatched out a revolver an saw Daggett swing his old head t drag out the old revolver that I ha While he swung it up, there was ti man like Alston to have fired aga times. I was about to break throug slaughter, when all at once I remer was only an acted scene—acted except old Daggett. He was in tl

of e mar

Al floo stag the still red hanc he'd from

As for a coat

"I he s forek wret this.

All front end, Dagg this wild turne

"M what name

She

how much this thing cost. More than a hundred thousand, I should say. A hundred thousand in one sparkler. Ah, Martha, you and Alston truly have high stakes on the table. Very high." He looked across at Alston and tried to smile, but it was a terrible poor excuse for a smile that he worked up.

"More of them, too," he said, "a great many more. Why, Martha, you've let yourself in for your share of a very tidy fortune, here. A great deal more than I could offer you at present it seems. A great deal more." His smooth voice warbled a bit, here, and his hand went up to his wrinkled old throat. He went on: "I see no good reason why I should not take these jewels and the rest, which belong to me, and try to ascertain if they may not have been stolen . . . as mine were about to be. Do you think of any good reason to advance against this, Alston?" And he scooped the stuff all together and raked it into the chamois bag.

"Will you look at me, Martha?" he said. "Poor girl, are you really going to give up everything and go off with a rascally gambler like Alston? Alston of all the men in the world. How will you be considered in the East, after this is known? You should know . . . because that world means a great deal more to you than it could ever mean to me."

He put the chamois bag into his pocket, and, as

he did that, Alston barked at him: "Daggett, drop that bag on the table, do you hear me? Put it back where you found it!"

"You speak harshly," Daggett said, looking more at Lou, believing she was his wife, than at Alston.

"I mean business," said Alston. "Your own stuff you may take out, but the rest has no concern of yours attached to it."

"How can I be sure of that?" Daggett asked gravely. "I tell you that the property of every honest man is the concern of every other honest man. And how can I tell that these sparklers really belong to you . . . and to Martha?"

"No other person has claimed them," Alston said.

"I claim them, then," said Daggett, "until the law decides otherwise."

"Daggett!" barked Alston, raising his voice sharp and hard.

"Don't do it," Daggett said, shaking his head in a sort of a sad fashion. "Don't bring out your gun, Alston. I warn you that this evening I am armed. And the truth of what will happen here is revealed to me . . . I cannot say by what marvelous foresight. But if you draw your weapon, I shall shoot you through the head and leave you dead on this floor . . . stretched beside the table, there. I have seen it all in a vision, Alston, and the very manner of your fall. I beg you in the name of heaven, believe what I am telling you. You have planned too much harm against me already, and you are given into my hands now. Will you believe me, Alston?"

Alston, backed into the farthest corner of the room, swayed a little from side to side, and it was wonderful to see the way he made fear and shame and a pretended desire for those faked jewels fight in his face. But finally, he said: "Well, let it go. I only want you to realize, Daggett, that you are changing parts with me, and becoming the real robber where I was only trying to be a robber. And what the law will say to you . . ."

"I shall be very willing to meet the law face to face," Daggett said, "quite as willing . . . or perhaps a little more so . . . than you can be. But . . ." He broke off, then added: "I have warned you, Alston. Beware of me!"

"Curse you and your warnings," Alston said. "And take this!"

He snatched out a revolver and fired, and I saw Daggett swing his old head to the side and drag out the old revolver that I had seen before. While he swung it up, there was time for a handy man like Alston to have fired again half a dozen times. I was about to break through and stop the slaughter, when all at once I remembered that this was only an acted scene—acted by everybody except old Daggett. He was in the deadest sort of earnest. He brought his old gun down on the mark and fired.

Alston let his Colt drop with a clatter to the floor, and he clasped his hands over his head and staggered forward. He pitched on his face beside the table and twisted over on his back and lay still in a sprawling shape, with a great smear of red down his face and through his hair, and in his hand I could see the little red sponge with which he'd done the trick—in or under his hand, away from the view of Daggett.

As for Daggett, he stood up, stiff and straight for a minute, and then dropped the gun into his coat pocket.

"I knew it would happen exactly like this," he said quietly. "I knew it with a very strange foreknowledge. Martha, God have pity on your wretched soul, because you were the cause of this. You were the cause of this . . ."

All at once there was a heavy knocking at the front of the house. It made my hair stand on end, and it seemed to throw a terrible chill into Daggett. He had been as calm as could be, up to this point, but now he went off the handle in a wild way, throwing his hands above his head. He turned into a child, very pitiful to see.

"Martha!" he yelled. "What shall I do? Oh, what shall I do? Help me, Martha, in heaven's name! Help me, I pray you!"

She only flung herself out of her chair, without

giving him a chance to see her face, and kneeled beside Alston.

And I could see Alston's lips move as he said: "Good, girl. Well done. Well done."

"You treacherous devil!" groaned Daggett. "The whole world is against me, and I have killed a man . . ."

He turned and plunged from the room just as the knock in the front part of the house was repeated. At the same time, the shadowy shape of a man that had been kneeling in front of the window jumped up and turned around toward me with a grunt of excitement. I gave him something that I had prepared for him a long time before— the long barrel of my Colt slammed along the side of his head so that I thought that I could feel the skull spring and bend under the shock. He gave one gasp and flopped on his face onto the floor of the balcony, just as old Alston, within the room, scrambled to his feet and started to say: "Honey, you worked it like a fine actress. And now if Carberry . . ."

Here he heard the gasp from the balcony and turned his head sharply toward us. "What's that?" he snarled. "Go and see, Lou. Because if . . ."

I didn't wait to hear any more. I dropped from my place and shinnied down the pillar and dropped to the ground. As I jumped away, a gun spurted fire above me, and a bullet almost tagged my head. It was Alston, standing on the balcony and raging like a madman, because I suppose he saw now that this fine scheme of his, the deepest and the smartest that ever any crook ever invented, was now wasted and all gone to pot.

However, I didn't have any chance to stand there and think these things out. I just ducked around the corner of the house and out of range of that barking gun of his, and, as I ran, I jerked out my own Colt again. A right good thing I did, too.

XX

All the devil had broken loose around that house, I can tell you. I heard someone shouting, off in the woods, and then there was the sudden roaring of a pair of guns in the basement of the house, and then the scream of a man in a terrible lot of agony. Dying, I supposed—because the scream ended, quick and short and sharp.

I ran straight on, beginning to wish that I was well out of this mess, and wondering how long it would be before Grenville and his gang jumped the house and scooped up everybody that was in it. And just as I got that idea, I saw a door open in the bottom of the house where I had never known that there had been a door before. I watched that door open, and a man run out into the trees.

Sort of by instinct, I yanked up my gun to be ready for trouble, but this gent ran straight past me, and I saw that it was old Daggett. He had his gun in one hand, and he had the chamois bag in the other, and, though he passed within a few feet of me, he didn't seem to guess that I was there.

He ducked into the trees, but, after he had gone a step or two, he stooped, and he jerked up what looked to me like a stone that weighed half a ton. He jerked that stone up and threw the bag in under it, and then he turned around and he ran back to the house and entered in through the side door. And that door closed after him, and there was the side of the house looking just as it had looked before.

The noise had all died down, too. I felt almost as though I had been dreaming these things, and had waked up like a sleepwalker.

The first thing I did was to run to that big-looking stone and lay hold of it. No, it was only a surface slab, and it came up, light and easy, in my hand. I picked out the chamois bag, but when I did that, my hand touched something else in there. I lit a match and looked.

It was the rotted shred of something that looked as though it might've been chamois in its day. But it was rotted by dampness and time, and its contents were spilled out onto the gravel. I saw that there was a collection of jewels like those that had been on the table in the room upstairs just a little time before. Well, it let in light on my slow head, at last. I saw the thing in one great crash.

In those old days, Alston had come to this house carrying with him loot that he got by stealing or by gambling. You couldn't hardly tell which. And he had aimed to collect pretty Martha Daggett— just as he had aimed to collect Lou Wilson, this next time. And he had been about to walk away with the girl and the jewels when in steps old Daggett—who maybe had come back early from a journey, and Daggett had spoiled everything. He had shot down Alston, and he had run down through the house.

Nobody knew where he had gone. They took it for granted that he had hidden the loot in the lower part of the old house, and that was the reason they had searched and searched. But why they hadn't simply torn the house to bits in the search was because this treasure was such a damned small handful that nobody could very well hope to find it if the house was turned into débris. So finally the grand scheme had come into the head of Alston when he saw, in Denver, a girl that had the same sort of features that Martha Daggett had had.

He had come out here, and he had staged this thing, fixing up the house and getting it all ready so that it would look just the way the place had looked in the old days—or near enough to the way that it had looked to fool a half-witted old man. And then everything was rehearsed just the way it had turned out on that other night—except that this time there was to be a close watch on where Daggett ran, and what he did with the sparklers.

And that was where this here fine scheme had broken down. Perhaps that scream that I had heard in the house explained a part of it. But anyway, the gent or the gents that were to watch where Daggett ran had lost out. And only by chance I had come onto the spot where the old man put the loot.

I thought this out in half a dozen seconds, while I was taking up the jewels. And then, as I cupped them in my hand, I wondered who there was in the world that would take them away from me—excepting the part of them that belonged to Daggett, and which I swore should go back into his hands and to nobody else's.

There were other parts of the whole thing that I didn't understand at all. And among the rest of it, I couldn't make out just where Buck Logan fitted in, because he was certainly more than a mere overseer of the work on the house. Neither could I tell where Carberry belonged, and I half suspected that I would never know, because Alston had promised the girl that she would never see the face of the old bandit. Then there were the Grenvilles. How did they come into the picture?

Well, time would take care of all of that, I thought. Then I decided that the first thing I should have to do was to go find Daggett. I wanted to get Lou out of this mess, but I felt somehow that no matter what happened, Lou would be pretty well able to take care of herself. Old Daggett, he was a different matter.

How he had managed to get clear of the house in spite of the rest of them, I couldn't tell. It was beyond me how he had been able to fool old

Alston and such a sharp fellow as Buck Logan, but the fact was that nobody had seen him leave the house, and maybe no one had seen him enter it again.

No, maybe I was wrong, after all, for just as I was about to start toward the house, I saw the same section of the bottom of the wall swing open like a door, and three men came sneaking out. They came slowly up toward the woods, playing a strong light over the ground.

"This is the way he came. No doubt about that. I could swear to these footsteps," said a voice that I thought I knew.

A moment later, as they came closer, I heard him say again. "Here he went, running all the way. Who would have thought there was such life in the old chap?"

I recognized the voice for certain, this time. It was Henry Grenville.

"Then how come that he turned around and went back into the house?" one of the other two asked.

"Maybe we'll find that out in turn," said Henry Grenville. "The first thing is to run down these tracks."

"What a mess Logan is, eh?" said another of the three. "Never seen a face like his."

"And he hollered loud enough," another said.

"He had reason, poor devil," Grenville said. "He had very good reason. I don't think he'll ever see the light of day again. He's paid for his part in this game."

"Blind forever."

"Yes, I had a good look at his eyes. They're ruined."

That was a shock for me, but hardly as much as the next thing I heard.

"Maybe he deserves what he got," one of Grenville's helpers said.

And Grenville himself answered, quick and sharp: "Deserves what he got? That devil deserved to be burned alive, inch by inch. There never was such a scoundrel since the world began. Even that Alston is a white man . . . almost a saint, compared with . . . Logan."

Well, I had traveled with Buck, bunked with him, cooked for him, eaten with him, and pretty near done everything except fight with him, and I couldn't see why he came in for any such talk as this, which was pretty sweeping, as you have to admit. But there was no doubt that there must've been something in what Grenville said, because he wasn't the sort of a man to say things rashly. He was a man who would have reasons for what he said, and that had a lot of weight with me.

Well, I watched the three of them follow up that trail, talking softly to each other, all the way, until they came to the spot where the big, flat-topped rock was.

146

"Here the trail ends . . . try that rock," said Grenville.

Then, in a minute I heard a deep chorus of voices, partly discouraged and partly excited, and I knew that they had found the place and they understood what it meant.

"Here's one stone . . . one diamond," Grenville said presently. "Some fox has been here before us. Now, let's find the man."

XXI

Well, I could have cursed myself properly to think that I had waited there until Grenville and his men came to that conclusion. If I jumped up and started running now, they would be sure to spot me, and, though it was a dark night, they had a spotlight to show them where to shoot.

"This way," I heard Grenville saying. "See how short his steps were. He was lighting matches, here, and looking at the loot."

By this time I was working my way out of that clump of brush that had looked so good to me and so safe to me a little time before. I got into the clear, but it took me a terrible lot of time, for I had to feel my way along in the pitch dark, and treat every limb of the bush as though it were a bottle of nitroglycerine. But clear I was, at the last—and I got up on my hands and knees and sneaked off a little ways until I thought it might be safe to stand on my two feet.

Just as I was about to sneak off at a run for the corner of the house, there was a sudden flash of light that fell across me from their spotlight.

"Mind your footing," snapped Grenville.

But one of the others called in an excited voice: "Did you see that? Who was that?"

"Where?"

"There! There he goes!"

I was up and away, but, as I jumped into full speed, their light steadied and shot full at me. I dodged out of the path of it as I heard Grenville sing out: "Willis! It's Willis! I might have guessed he would be on the inside when the crash came. Boys, if you down him, we are rich!"

They found me with that flickering light again, and three guns smashed at the same time. I felt a bullet knife through the upper part of my left arm, and then I turned the corner of that house a little faster than a running deer when the hounds give tongue behind it. They followed as fast as they could, but they would have needed wings to get me, after that.

I had intended to cut off toward the woods. But by the hot spurt of the blood down my side, I knew that I needed help, and that I needed it quick and bad. I rounded to the front of the place, leaped up onto the porch, and kicked open the front door.

I slammed it behind me in time to have it splintered from top to bottom by two or three bullets. And at the same time I heard two voices shouting in the bottom part of the house, and then two guns sounded in quick exchange.

After that there was silence again. No one seemed to be stirring on the outside of the place. And on the inside there was a terrible dead silence for another moment—then I heard a faint groaning from the bottom part of the house.

Well, I glanced down to that arm of mine and I knew that I would have to find a friend and find one quick. So I put my head back and shouted: "Lou! Lou Wilson! D'you hear?"

I waited another minute. A door slammed somewhere.

Then: "Hello! Doc?"

That was the voice of Lou, and nothing ever sounded half so good to me as her voice when she was singing out. I went up the stairs three at a time, and I found her on the landing above. She grabbed me.

"What's happened? What has happened?" she gasped.

"I don't know half," I said, "but just now the main thing is for you to leave go of my left arm. It's been hurt and I want you to tie it up for me."

"Here's the hospital," Lou said. "Come in with me."

She took me into the same room where she had been sitting with Alston when things began to happen. Alston wasn't there now. But young Grenville sat in a chair in one corner of the room, slumped far back, his eyes closed, and a bandage tied around his head and passing over a part of his face. I didn't have to ask how he had got that. It was where the long, cold, heavy barrel of the Colt had landed when I knocked down the man

150

who had been with me on the balcony outside of the window.

But Larry Grenville wasn't alone there. Lou was right in calling it the hospital. At the table there was a big hulk of a man sitting with his face in his arms, and his arms resting on the table. By the wide look of his shoulders I knew that it was Buck Logan. He raised his head. There was a bandage right straight across his eyes, and I guessed that Harry Grenville had been right when he said that Buck was blinded.

"What happened, Buck?" I asked.

"Plenty," he said as cool as you please. "How are things with you, kid? You'll have to tell me. I'm through with seeing for myself."

"It's not as bad as that," I told him. "It sure can't be as . . ."

There was a little cry from Lou, here, because she had got my sleeve cut away and she was seeing the wound and the blood that was welling out of it. But she didn't make any fuss. She went right on like a brave girl, and began to tidy up that wound, and then to put a dressing on it.

"It's as bad as all that, though," replied Buck. "I'm a gone goose, kid."

"What happened?"

"I was down in the cellar, waiting till Alston had scared old Daggett that way. And when he came, like a fool, I let him see me. I forgot that he had a gun with him."

"A gun loaded with blanks," I said. I remembered the sound of the shot that Daggett had fired at Alston when that crook pretended to fall dead under it.

"Loaded with blanks, yes," Buck agreed. "But when a blank is fired close enough, what happens? Think of a cat spitting fire."

Well, that was enough to tell me what I wanted to know. You watch the spurt of a Colt fired in the night and you know what I mean. The jump of the fire goes quite a little distance, and I knew that the burning grains of powder had spurted into the eyes of Buck Logan. I remembered, too, that the scream that I had heard from the bottom part of the house not long before old Daggett had come running out. And that was it. It was the yell of Buck when that torment was shot into his face. It was enough to break even his nerve, though that was stronger than good-proved steel.

Well, I had had a good many doubts about Buck, but when I saw him sitting there so quiet and so calm, I had to put a hand on his shoulder, and say: "Buck, old-timer, I'm sure sorry. I'm mighty sorry. But the doctors these days can fix up pretty near anything, and they'll fix up you, too. Wait and see, you'll be all right."

He smiled. Have you ever seen a man smile when his eyes are covered? Leastwise, with Buck, it was like watching the grin of a wolf.

"I've got what's coming to me," Buck said. "I don't whine. I'm finished. But when you get your arm tied up, will you do one last thing for me, Doc?"

"Sure," I answered.

"Thanks. It'll be about the last thing that I got to ask from anybody, I suppose. But go down and find Alston. He'll be around in the lower part of the house, messing about. Get Alston and bring him back up here. But don't say that it's me that wants him. I got to have a talk with him. You hear?"

"Sure, and I'm fixed up fine right now."

I got downstairs, and I turned to the cellar door, and through it I soft-footed for the cellar beneath, because there was where I was most likely to find Alston, according to what Buck had said. There I found him, too, being led to him by a faint glow of a lantern.

He was too busy with his work to pay any attention to me. He was working away at the wall, taking out stone after stone as quick as he could free it from the cement. And already he had cleared away enough to show a great gaping hole—a hole that led not outside into the night, but into a vacancy between the two walls that had been built there. It looked pretty ghostly, but I could remember how old Daggett had seemed to walk out of the solid side of the house, and I could guess what Alston was after.

And Daggett? I thought he was asleep, at first, for he lay on his back, stretched out so peaceful, with his eyes closed. But then I saw the purple splotch at the side of his head, and something about the stillness and the stiffness was enough to make me understand—even though I hadn't stopped to think that he wouldn't be lying down here asleep on the cold cellar floor,

No, he wasn't sleeping. He was dead. I remembered the two shots and the groan. Alston must have done the rotten thing, though I couldn't see how even Alston could ever get as low-down as to do a murder like that one.

I slipped up behind him and put the cold mouth of my Colt against his neck. He sagged forward and drew in his breath with a bubbling sound. "Get up, you coyote," I hissed.

He waited half a second. "Willis," he said.

"Maybe," I said.

"Curse the day that ever made Logan hire you," he said. "What do you want with . . . ?"

"Don't turn around, but put your hands up good and high. I sure like to see them that way . . . as though you're holding up the roof from falling. That's just the way I like to see you, old-timer."

"All right," he said. "But why all the fuss?"

"I don't know," I said. "I was sent for you."

"Did Logan send you?" he asked, quick and sharp.

"No," I lied. "You've asked enough questions, and now I'll ask a couple. What happened to old Daggett?"

He didn't even bother trying to deny it. "Silly old fool was stubborn. He irritated me too much. Where do you want me to go?"

"March ahead of me," I said, "with your hands up all the way. Poor old Daggett. I tell you, Alston, I'm aching and yearning and longing to kill you. I hope you'll give me a fair excuse. And I'll tell you this . . . you're the first man I've ever met that I'd as soon shoot through the back as through the face. You hear me talk?"

He heard me, and a little wriggle ran down his back as the chilly idea that I was all in earnest went to his black heart. Then he marched on ahead of me without a word.

I herded him up the stairs. And only when he came to the door of the room where the rest were, did he hesitate a little as he looked at Logan.

"Good," said Logan.

But I looked chiefly at the girl, and her face was a study of disgust and contempt as she eyed Alston.

"Not even dangerous . . . to a man," she said.

"Here he is, Buck," I announced. "And now, old boy, what do you want with him? He's got his hands up in the air."

"Oh, none of that," Buck said. "Him and me are friends for too long to need anything like that. I want him to sit down here, close to me. That's all. Set him down in a chair close to me."

I told Alston to do what was ordered, and, when he sat down, Buck put out a big brown hand and gathered in one of the wrists of Alston. And I saw a shudder go through Alston's body. He was a pretty sick-looking fellow, if ever I saw one.

"Gents," I said, "I dunno what's in the air here, but I got to tell you this. Here is Alston, the only fit gent that we got left . . . and Grenville and his bunch are all outside, raving and tearing to get inside this here house because they know that the jewels of Daggett are here."

"How do they know that?" snapped Alston.

"How do we know that they're here?" I asked, sneering.

"Forget about the jewels, Al," Buck said. "Hear me chatter, will you?"

XXII

"Well," Buck said, "I'll only keep the attention of you gents for a few minutes. I want to tell you about a couple of boys. One was a bad boy that used to punch the noses of the other boys in the school. And one was a good boy that was always at the head of his class and that was so smart that he knew how to have his fun and always shift the blame of it onto the head of the bad boy. And yet when there came a pinch, he always knowed how to make the bad boy his friend, and to use him."

"Buck . . . ," Alston said, getting white.

"Never mind, old-timer," Buck said. And he began to pat and stroke the hand of Alston that he was holding. I felt that something pretty dreadful was in the offing, but I couldn't guess what.

"Well," Buck continued, "the bad boy left the school. Run away . . . and he didn't go back no more. But a long spell later on, when he was a young buckaroo, he meets up with the good boy. Says the good boy . . . 'There is lots of gold in the camps, kid. I'll go inside and work them with the cards. You stay on the outside and work them with your gang. I'll feed you the information that you need all the time. And you and me will split up the profits, understand?'

"Well, the bad boy thought that this was pretty

good. He done the thing. The good boy played cards and got the information, and he passed it out to the bad boy. And the bad boy, he got into the swing of holding up gold shipments and having a good time all around. And being bad, he had fights. And being a steady hand, when he had a fight, he most generally did a little killing. You understand?"

Oh, I understood, well enough. We were hearing the inside history of Alston and somebody else—and the name of Carberry was the one that was behind my teeth. I would've given a lot of money to know how Buck came to hear all of this stuff.

"Finally they made a big pot," went on Buck.

" 'What are we gonna do with this stuff?' the bad boy asked.

" 'Turn it into jewels. They bulk down even smaller than banknotes,' says the good boy, who had a pretty wise head on his shoulders.

"So they each turned their half into jewels, and they met up and counted over the shiners what they had collected and admired each other and the size of the pile that they had got together.

"The bad boy, he proposed a drink. And the good boy said that it was a damned good idea, and first he slipped a little pinch of knock-out drops into the booze of the bad boy. And after the bad boy had taken the drink, he gave a yawn and went to sleep.

"The good boy took all of the loot and

disappeared. And the bad boy, he pretty near died from the effects of that stuff, because the good boy had meant to kill him with the poison . . . and nothing saved the bad boy from dying except getting powerful sick.

"Well, when the bad boy got his senses and his health back, he says to himself that he has been bad for a long time, and killed his men and done a lot of damage, and here he winds up in the end with a good chance of getting himself hanged, should the news of him ever leak out. But he decided that he would now try his hand at going straight. So he got himself a new name and a string of mules and started being honest. And he thanked heaven that his face wasn't known, tied to the name of Carberry."

The cat was out of the bag, now.

Alston gave a gasp, and said: "You idiot, Buck . . . what do you mean?" And he reached back to his hip pocket.

"Steady, Alston," I said. "Remember what I told you while we were coming up the stairs."

And I tilted my gun down and watched him through the sights—not a pretty picture, either.

Buck went drawling on: "But after I had gone straight for a long time and begun to respect myself and the rest of the world, pretty much, along comes Alston and says to me . . . 'Carberry, this is the time for us to make a grand clean-up. Point your gun the other way. It won't do you any good to kill me now because I tried to kill you and did rob you that other time. The thing for you to know is that the stuff I stole from you I lost afterward. And more besides. Your stuff, Carberry, and mine . . . and the Grenville jewels that I lifted and had along with me . . . and the gems I polished off a chap by name of Daggett. This here Daggett was about to lose his stuff through his wife, when he popped up, shot me down, and then went mad and lost the stuff where he himself couldn't find it. But I have the world's greatest scheme for making Daggett himself lead us to that loot. And a grand big fortune it is."

Alston put in with a sort of a scream: "He lies! He lies like the very devil!"

"But in this deal," said Buck Logan, alias Carberry, "I've collected my finish. And now, Alston, you've come to your finish, too." And as he said that, he yanked at his clothes and brought out a Colt that looked about a yard long to me and black as a bucket of paint.

Alston screamed like a wild man and jumped up and snatched out his own weapon. He fired first, and Buck sank onto his knees, a dying man. He still had hold of Alston's hand, though Alston was screaming and fighting to get away. And Buck dragged him closer and reached out his Colt until the muzzle of it got to the body of Alston. Then he fired twice.

I got to him in time to knock up his hand after

the second shot, but I was a long, long time too late. Alston dropped dead, and Buck sagged down on the floor, his big head wagging from side to side.

I forgot everything except the jolly old days when we'd followed the mules up the trail toward the valley. I forgot all the lies and the double-crossing.

"Buck," I said.

"Is he dead?" Buck asked.

"Yes," I told him, "and for the killing of him you pretty near deserve a reward, Buck."

"The reward I deserve is what I'll get," he said. "Shake hands with me, kid. And remember this here one thing, will you? That the white man you knowed by the name of Buck Logan was white, though his name wasn't Logan, and . . ."

He died there, and I felt the strength go out of his big hand. But I couldn't see his dead face. There were too many tears in my eyes.

Which would prove that even a Carberry could be loved by a friend, but nobody on God's earth would ever dream of grieving for half a minute for that rat Alston. Or for any of his kind.

Now that Buck is finished, there doesn't seem much energy in me for telling the rest. Because, really, the rest was all happiness.

Before we left that house, we had to make a dicker with the gang of Grenville—I mean that Lou and me did—that we would let the first sheriff be the umpire. The first sheriff was. He came and saw the house and he heard the story. He took the loot and groaned.

"Why wasn't I born to be a crook?" he said. And then he turned around and put me in jail.

Well, that was just his way of seeing that I got justice, and I sure had plenty of it before I got through. For five months they see-sawed up and down, until they finally got it clear in their heads that I hadn't killed anybody.

By that time Lou and me was only waiting to get married. And by that time the jewels had been gone over. Larry and Henry Grenville were able to pick out the stuff that had belonged in their family. And other folks turned up here and there to make their claims.

Yes, plenty of claims, and nine-tenths of them crooked. But all that had any sort of proof got their stuff back. And the rest—about a third of the stuff that we had brought in—was turned over to Lou and to me, and we made it a wedding present. She had her doubts about starting our lives on blood money, but I tried to convince her that she had no right to complain, because, if it hadn't been for us, everything would have been lost to the world. And, to make amends for anything that was tainted in that coin, we made our decision to start right in where poor old Daggett had left off.

And that was what we did. It took ten years

of hard work. It meant sinking money by the tens of thousands. But across that desert we ran a road that nobody would be ashamed to travel on. And the railroad got interested and ran up a branch line to the creek. And we cleared the big meadows, and we fed the big trees—or a handy part of them—into the sawmills.

I dunno that this here job has really paid, and I figure that if we had put the money out at five percent in the first place, it would've done a lot more for us in the meantime—but, just the same, we never regret it.

Because, between you and me, we feel that old Daggett himself must know about what's happening, and that it would sure tickle him to see the valley prosper the way it has under us.

The old house is gone. There was too much sorrow in its roots, as you might say. And we put us up a big, rambling, careless sort of a log house. But the kids like it, and we like it. And Daggett Creek comes winding and singing and shining right past under our windows. So what more could a body ask?

RODEO RANCH

I

It happened to *Señor Don* Ramon Alvarez in the following manner. He was deep in the first sleep of the night and in the middle of the first happy dream when he wakened suddenly. He heard nothing and saw nothing in the blackness of the room, yet he knew perfectly that he was in the greatest danger. So he lay still, concentrating upon the problem. Reason told him that his house was large, his servants many, and the probability of danger reaching him in his own room remote indeed, but when he struggled the hardest to assure himself of his safety, at that very moment instinct protested that he was wrong and that death was stalking softly toward his bed.

He turned his head toward the wall and the door. He could see nothing except those strange, formless objects that sift about in the darkness for those who stare hard enough and long enough into the blank space. He reached up and under his pillow. He found the butt of the revolver and squeezed it with a huge relief. In fact, if there were an actual danger confronting him, he would not perish unavenged. Thus he assured himself as he lay there with the perspiration standing upon his forehead and his heart pounding like the thud of a racer's hoofs.

Then at the very moment when he had almost conquered his terror, he received the indubitable proof. For a hand touched him upon the breast, a soft and gliding touch. Still there was nothing to be seen in the darkness above him, and there was not a sound to be heard, but Alvarez, with a strong twist of his body, whirled himself out from under the danger, whatever it might be, and rolled by a complete turn nearer to the window. The cat that darts up and away as the shadow of the dog slides near moves not more quickly than did *Don* Ramon. And even so the blow missed him by a scant fraction of an inch. The bedclothes were twisted tightly around his body. He heard the hiss of a blade that thrust its length into the mattress. He heard the faint grunt of one who has wasted a mighty effort, and then he fired into nothingness.

There was no shout of pain or protest, not even the patter of feet in flight. Far away in the house rolled the echo of the explosion, but still there was no sound of human voice. Small wonder that an assassin had come with a knife to hunt him, seeing that he was so insecurely guarded. Would it be hours before the dull-wits, the blockheads, had heard that gun and realized what it meant? Would it be hours before they rushed to his rescue? He could have been killed a hundred times before their efforts could have saved him or gotten revenge for him.

He fired again, with a wild panic starting in his brain, and the flash of the second shot showed him the work of the first. The body of a man was sprawled upon the foot of the bed, lying inert, limp, lifeless, as he knew by even that fraction of a second's glance.

Alvarez jumped from the bed and snapped on the electric light. And now he turned at last toward his victim and assailant. He went to the bed and leaned over. The dead man lay upon his face, his hands thrown straight above his head, and in the left hand was the knife that had already been thrust into the bedding in the search for the body of Alvarez. It was a tawny, long-fingered hand with a big emerald on the third finger, a flat-faced emerald upon which was incised a delicate design.

When Alvarez saw that design, he whimpered softly and turned his head over his shoulder. If anyone had come through the door at that instant, he would have seen a face that was a veritable mask of tragedy and fear. The eyes were starting forth; the lips were drawn tight and were trembling; his nostrils expanded; his cheeks were sagging. He had grown, of a sudden, ten years older.

Such was the face that Alvarez turned toward the door. He ran to it and turned the key in the lock. Then back he raced to the prostrate form in the bed, and, seizing it by the shoulder, he turned it over. He found himself looking down into wide, dull eyes, and upon the lips there was a crushed smile of foolish derision. Alvarez, however, had no regard for the smile. He was only interested in the features. It was a long, lean face. A habitual frown made a crease, even in death, between the eyes. The face was as yellow tan as the hands. Plainly he was not a white American. There was the smoke of Indian blood in that complexion, and in the yellow-stained pupils of the eyes.

Alvarez looked upon the dead man with a peculiar horror. He went backward at a staggering pace and fell into the arms of a big, overstuffed chair. He slumped into it so inertly that his head struck heavily against the thick roll at the back of the chair, and he sat there with his eyes riveted upon the wall before him as though he saw the picture of his fate drawn in the clearest outline before him.

He passed his hand hastily through his hair. It was a dense mass of the thickest silver, and it stood up almost on end after the gesture, giving him an unwonted appearance of wildness and dissipation.

Now came footfalls down the hall. How long had it been since that report from the revolver should have roused the household? It seemed a quarter of an hour to Alvarez, although perhaps excitement had lengthened seconds to minutes for him. He heard a hand turn the knob of the door.

Then there was a shout of fear when it failed to open. Others took up the cry, up and down the hall. Perhaps there were a score of tongues in the shout: "They've murdered the master and locked his door! The *señor* is dead!"

Alvarez grinned at the door mirthlessly and shook his clenched fist at it, like one who suffers so much that he is glad to see anxiety in others. Then he hastened back to the limp figure upon the bed. He tore the ring from the third finger of the left hand, looked down with a shudder to the diagram upon the face of the emerald, and dropped it in his pocket. Then he went in the greatest haste through the pockets of the deceased. There was a wallet, stuffed with papers and with plenty of currency. Certainly hunger and pressing poverty could not have impelled the stranger to the crime that he had attempted, for there was something over $1,000 in that wallet. And had he been in need, he might have raised several thousand more upon the emerald, for it was a stone as large and splendid as it was strangely cut. And it was strange indeed to find a jewel so precious, cut as a seal.

Alvarez shoved the wallet under his pillow. In the other pockets of the stranger he discovered nothing of importance. There were cigarettes, a few cigars—thick at the fire end after the Mexican style—and a heavy pocket knife mounted in gold, but without any identifying initials. All of these things Alvarez left in the clothes of the stranger. Then he turned to the door of his bedroom against which his servants were thundering. He strode to it and cast it wide open, with the result that he nearly received half a dozen bullets in the face, so convinced were his adherents that he was dead and that only his murderer could be living in the room.

They gave back with lowered guns and with yells of joy when they saw that it was Alvarez himself who stood before them. The cook fell upon his knees and threw up his hands in thanksgiving, so that Alvarez was touched, and it took a great deal indeed to move Alvarez.

Yet he would not allow his gentler feelings to control him. As they stood before him, he scowled heavily, and let them have the full advantage of his expression before he uttered a word. Then it was to shout at them: "Traitors! Blockheads! Fools! Have you left me here to be massacred while you slept in your beds? I have fed you and clothed you and treated you like my children. I have squandered my money upon you. I have given you all a home. And now I am left here to be murdered in my bed!"

They drew together in a frightened huddle under his torrent of abuse, which was freely interspersed and sprinkled with oaths. They began to protest that the instant they heard the explosion of the gun in the room of the master, they had come at once to his rescue, but he shut them off with more curses.

At length he bade them come in and view the villain who would have destroyed his life, and they trooped in together, whispering and gasping with horror until they found the body upon the bed. Then they were speechless, and with that as an object lesson before them, Alvarez read to them a long lecture upon the beauties of honest and faithful service to an overgenerous master, for, like some other employers of labor, Alvarez appreciated his own virtues to the uttermost.

He drove them out, at length, and sent some of them to find the coroner and others to find the sheriff. He himself went back into the bedroom and spent a few minutes walking up and down, up and down, his face twisted with anxiety. It was not the man lying upon the bed to whom he gave a thought. It was rather the presence of some danger in the outer world that troubled him and that caused him, now and again, to pause at one of the big windows and shake his fist at the possibilities that lay somewhere between him and the misty circle of the horizon.

When the sheriff arrived, he found the rich rancher dressed and in his library. The language of Alvarez was strange for a man who has recently escaped from the hands of a secret and midnight murderer, for he told the sheriff that he was sorry for the thing that he had been compelled to do that night. He was confident that no man would willingly assail the life of another man who had not injured him, and that there must have been some cause of great poverty and pressing need that had caused the stranger to invade his home. The sheriff replied with a grunt.

II

As a matter of course, Alvarez received nothing but praise for the adroitness with which he had baffled the murderer. It was surmised that the absence of any papers that might identify the stranger, as well as the removal of a ring from his finger—for the pale band was noted as well as the indentation in the flesh of the finger—indicated that the murderer, in taking his chance to kill the rich rancher, had purposely removed all possible means of identifying himself in case he should be killed in the attempt. As for the purpose of destroying Alvarez, it was instantly apparent, for around his neck Alvarez wore the key that opened the safe in which his money for current expenses was kept. And that money was enough to make a large haul.

But, on the whole, the attempt to destroy *Don* Ramon was considered lucky for the rest of the district, for it was the immediate cause of the celebration of a great festival by the rancher. He wished to indicate his joy at his escape, and for that reason he organized a rodeo that quite put in the shade other affairs of the kind.

There was one fault to be found with his plans, and that was that there was only a week's notice given. However, the instant his announcement was made it was carried in all the newspapers of the range towns, and four days were enough to bring in cowpunchers from the distant sections. Furthermore, the prizes were of such a nature that every skillful man along the range was sure to come if he possibly could, for *Don* Ramon had dipped deep into his pocket for the sake of the festival. There were handsome cash prizes for every event. And the events ranged from fancy roping to foot racing—from horse breaking to knife throwing—from boxing to shooting. There were events in which white men were sure to excel, and there were events in which Mexicans were certain to excel, and there were others in which the Indians would stand forth. Who but an Indian, for instance, could be expected to win a twenty-four-hour race across the desert and the mountains?

On the whole it would be a great spectacle, and people immediately began mustering for it. But, in the meantime, there was a single blot upon the happiness of the occasion, and that was the news that *Don* Ramon was confined to his bed, and that he might not be able to view the sports of the great day. The nature of his sickness was not known. Some held that it was the result of a nervous breakdown caused by the crisis through which he had just passed, and others, again, declared that the poor *don* was suffering merely from old age.

However that might be, *Don* Ramon did not leave his bed in the interim before the sports began. Neither did he rise on the morning of the festival, but sent his majordomo to distribute the prizes in his name. He stayed in his bed, attended by his doctors and surrounded by soft-footed servants. It was not until the late afternoon of the day that he arrived at the field. He came there, indeed, barely in time for the last and the greatest of all the contests. That was the shooting.

Ordinarily gun play held secondary place in such affairs, if it appeared at all, but on this occasion it was given a great emphasis by the prize that was offered. It was a prize calculated to attract every red-blooded cowpuncher who had ever had any skill with guns in his life. It was the sort of prize that made even the spectators yearn to be in the lists taking part in the trial of skill. In a word, the prize that *Don* Ramon was offering was his famous chestnut stallion, El Capitán. He was a six-year-old king among horses, and had been brought to the West especially to give *Don* Ramon's ranch an unequaled stock of finest horseflesh. El Capitán had cost the *don* a trip to England and many thousands of dollars. El Capitán, as *Don* Ramon christened the horse, was immediately considered an object of public pride by the entire community. Ever since it had been announced that he was to be the prize for the shooting, people had begun to wonder whether good *Don* Ramon had gone mad or whether the stallion was not so wonderful after all. The result was that for a week crowds had come to watch him in his corral.

El Capitán was not much under seventeen hands in height, but for all his bulk he was built like a picture horse. His gait was as light and mincing as any dancing pony's. His head was all that a horse's head should be, a very poem of beauty, courage, pride, and great-heartedness. And that this miracle among horses should be given as the prize in a shooting match was too strange to be true. *Don* Ramon was forced to give an explanation through his majordomo. His ranch was stocked with El Capitán's progeny, therefore it was possible for him to part with his favorite. But most of all he was giving the stallion to encourage marksmanship and practice with guns among the cowpunchers of the range, for he declared that the greatest of all frontier accomplishments was falling into disuse, and it was his ambition to help restore it. Beginning with this year he would offer an annual prize for the best shot in the West. And each prize would be almost as splendid as the one that he was offering this season.

This explanation was accepted for what it might be worth, but the cowpunchers were frankly incredulous. El Capitán was worth a small fortune. It was still incredible that he should be put up for the prize in a day's sport. However, having been carefully examined, he was pronounced without a single flaw. Altogether he was matchless. In England he had not been fast enough to keep up with the light-footed sprinters on the tracks, therefore he had not been of use either as a racer or as a sire of racers. But where the course was to last all day and where the track was not a smoothed turf but a wild way over mountains and sandy deserts, El Capitán kept going where other horses dropped beside the way.

The very best men in the country came to vie with one another in the contest. It was a strange struggle, unlike any that had ever been held before. It began with rifle shooting at close and at long range. It continued with rifle shooting at moving objects. And it closed with revolver work, and skill with the revolver counted against skill with the rifle as three is to one. For the revolver, said *Don* Ramon in his announcement, should be the unique weapon of the Western ranges.

All centered, then, upon adroitness with the smaller weapon. In the beginning the contestants were lined up and asked to try their skill upon stationary targets. These targets were large-headed nails driven into boards and placed at such a distance that they were almost invisible. Five men came through this contest. The others were hopelessly distanced. Then the five were required to shoot at bricks thrown into the air at a uniform height and distance, and when that part was over, they were made to mount their horses and ride at a gallop between two rows of posts on each of which a small can was placed. Those cans had to be blown off, and there was only one way in which it could be done. The horse must be controlled with the knees and the voice, and there must be a revolver in each hand.

The five set their teeth and prepared for the crucial test. They had weathered the brick shooting well enough. Shooting from the firm ground at a moving object was one thing but shooting from a moving object at a stationary one was quite another. The difference is that which exists between guns on shore and guns at sea. Everyone knows that a single large-caliber gun on land is equal to a whole battleship armed with a dozen such guns afloat in the sea.

So, with their horses prepared, their guns ready, the five awaited the signal. It was given, and Shorty Galbraith, famous in song and story in spite of his scant forty years, went gallantly down between the rows. His horse cantered with the rhythmical precision of a circus animal. It rocked slowly ahead, and from either hand Shorty blazed away at the cans. His bullets flicked off the first three pair. Then he began to miss with his left-hand gun and scored two blanks with his port weapon, a thing that so upset him that, with his last two shots, he missed on both sides. He had knocked off eight out of twelve cans, however, and that was a score amazingly high. It would be very strange if it were much improved upon by any of the remaining four champions. For Shorty was almost ambidextrous and could use his right hand almost as well as his left.

The applause that greeted Shorty's effort had hardly died down when old Chapman, hero of a score of fights in the old days and still as steady of eye and hand as ever, started for the posts. He scored a double miss on the first pair of posts. But the next four pair went off as if by magic, and exultant cheers were beginning from his supporters when he missed as completely on the last pair as he had missed on the first. However, he had tied with Shorty. And he reined his horse to one side, prepared heartily to wish bad luck to the remaining three contestants. Of these the first one to make the attempt failed almost completely. He knocked off one of the first pair, but then his horse started forward too fast, and he succeeded in bringing down only three of the remaining targets. But the marksman who followed called up an hysteria of cheering by actually bringing down nine of the cans. So loud was the yelling that the old fellow had to take off his hat to the thunder and wave it at his admirers. He was a veteran frontiersman, tall, lean, with a head on which flashed many a gray hair when he had removed his sombrero. His name was Sam Calkins, and though he was not as well-known as some of his competitors, his figure, his stately bearing, his grave and reserved manner of speech complied with all the traditions of the West. Everyone instantly wished him well, particularly because of the character of his single opponent who remained to rival his score.

The latter had won the disapproval of the crowd earlier in the match. In the first place, instead of the usual cowpuncher's outfit, he was dressed in riding trousers of neat whipcord, and his boots of soft, black leather were polished like two dark mirrors. The very hat upon his head was new, and instead of a wide-brimmed sombrero it was a close-brimmed affair that set jauntily a little upon one side of his head. He was set off with a red bowtie. But above all, instead of sitting in a true range saddle, he was mounted upon a smooth English affair, with short stirrups. But his manners had given even more offense than his clothes. He had joked and laughed through half of the contests. He was still smiling as he reined his horse toward the beginning of the double row of posts. And the crowd, with a scowl of cordial dislike, held its breath. Not that it actually thought that such a hero as the efficient Sam Calkins could be bested by this stranger who was so obviously not of the range, but because they dreaded even the hundredth chance. Moreover, everyone had to admit that Duds Kobbe, as they had nicknamed the stranger, had shot amazingly well hitherto.

He went to the starting point amidst loud yells of advice.

"Mind your necktie, Duds!"

"The girls are all lookin' at you, kid!"

"Your mamma'd be proud to see you, Duds!"

To this he responded with another of his laughs, and then started his horse down the gantlet, and with such careless speed that his rate of going was half again as great as that of any of the previous riders. And, seeing his nonchalance, the crowd waited with held breath, dreading, hoping.

Crash went his guns, and the first two cans were blown from the tops of the posts. He fired again, and the second pair went down. And the pace of his galloping horse had actually increased. Again he fired, and the third pair went down. Still he was not turning his head from side to side, but he rode with his face straight forward and seemed to be sighting his guns either from the corners of his eyes or by instinct. It was like wizardry.

There was a heavy groan of relief when he missed with his right-hand gun on the fourth pair. There was an actual shout when he failed with his left-hand Colt on the fifth. There remained the final pair. Men noticed in the interim that stanch Sam Calkins had not ceased rolling his cigarette, and that at the very instant of the crisis he was actually reaching for a match. He was upholding the good stoical Western tradition in the time-honored way.

Meanwhile, young Kobbe was at the final pair of posts. He shot the left-hand can cleanly from its post. He had tied Sam at the worst. And at the best he might yet . . .

The crowd refused to consider that possibility. The groan took an audible sound of a word: "Miss!"

And it seemed as if there were a magic in that wish. For when he fired his twelfth shot the can was not flicked from the post top. A loud yell of exultation rose from the crowd. However, that cry stopped in mid-breath, for the can had been grazed by the bullet and was rocking and tottering in its place. It reeled to one side. It staggered to the other and would have settled down in its place in quiet, as many of the bystanders afterward declared, had not a gust of wind of strange violence at this instant cuffed the can away and tumbled it to the ground!

III

There could not have been a stronger proof of the unpopularity of the stranger than the groan with which the crowd witnessed this piece of good fortune. But they were stunned by what followed. For Duds Kobbe, riding back from the conclusion of the trial, approached the judges, who were three old ranchers, now sour-faced with disappointment, and assured them that he would not accept a win that had been given him by the wind and chance rather than his own skill.

The judges could hardly believe their ears, and though in strict justice they should have awarded the prize to him and insisted that there should be no further contest, they were only human, and all three of them, if the truth must be admitted, had placed their money upon the celebrated Sam.

Sam had half-heartedly protested that he could not accept another chance since he had been fairly beaten, but in the middle of his protest he glanced across to the place where El Capitán was being held, and the sun at that instant flashed along the silken flanks of the great stallion. It was too much for Sam, and his protest died, half uttered. But the news of what had happened swept in stride through the crowd.

It was one of those things that make men shake

their heads and then see with new eyes. When they looked across to the shining form of the stallion as he turned and danced in the sunshine, and when they realized that a man had voluntarily given up that king of horses for the sake of some delicate scruple of conscience, they prepared to revise their opinions of the stranger. They looked at him through different eyes, and what they saw was something more than the oddness of his appearance. It had been impossible, up to this time, for the spectators to see anything in Duds Kobbe except his extraordinary clothes. Now they discovered that he was a fine-looking fellow, a shade under twenty-five years, straight, wide-shouldered, big-necked, spare of waist, and with long and sinewy arms. He was the very ideal of the athlete, as a matter of fact, and the closer they looked at him, the better they liked him.

If his skill with guns had not proclaimed him a man, his fine rich tan, his clear voice, and the manner in which he sat his saddle would have convinced the discerning that there was real metal in him. And when the two sat their horses at the beginning of the double row of posts, when the cans had been replaced, and when Sam had loaded his guns with infinite care, it would have been hard for the crowd to pick its favorite. Sam was a fine fellow, but he had showed himself a little too eager to accept the proffered generosity of the stranger. Kobbe had shown himself above and beyond all meanness.

Sam rode first, as before. He duplicated his original feat, knocking off nine of the cans, but Kobbe, riding down the line, actually blew eleven of the twelve from their places and was rewarded with a roar of applause from the bystanders.

The evening was growing heavy in the west when they brought Duds Kobbe to the chestnut horse. Instantly they were aware of anachronism. For El Capitán carried a heavy Western range saddle, and the winner of the prize was dismounting from an English pad. But they were left in doubt for only an instant. Duds Kobbe bounded down from the one horse and onto the back of the other without pause. He swept off his hat and slapped El Capitán across the neck with it and at the same time pricked him with the spurs.

Never before had the great stallion been treated in such fashion. He had been surrounded by tenderness all of his days. Now he was used like a common range pony. He tried first to jump into the center of the sky. Then he strove to knock a hole in the earth with his hoofs and stiffened legs. After that he passed through a frantic maze of bucking, only to come out on the farther side, so to speak, with his rider as happy in the saddle as ever, still slapping him with the annoying hat, still tickling his sides with the spurs. El Capitán stopped, shook his head, and looked back to consider this strange puzzle in the saddle upon his back.

So the contest ended and passed into legend. The legend grew until it reached amazing proportions, and to this day they will tell the curious stranger how Duds Kobbe tossed his revolvers into the air and caught them again between every shot.

But when Duds was riding off the field, surrounded by laughing, shouting, good-natured men, a dark-faced fellow approached him from the side and rode close.

"*Señor* Alvarez," he said, "is eager to see *Señor* Kobbe," and with that he turned and rode away. Kobbe, as soon as he could be rid of his well-wishers and had shaken hands with Sam, who buried his disappointment behind a smile, turned the head of the chestnut toward the house of Alvarez.

He did not stay for the feast at which all the other participants gathered that night, where the long tables were spread with food enough for all the villagers and all the spectators. They were served with the meat of steers roasted whole, to say nothing of scores of kids, fresh from the spits where they had been faithfully turned by the sons and daughters of the ranch hands on the wide lands of Alvarez. There were chickens and geese stewed in immense pots over open fires. In fact, people were staggered when they thought of the amount of money that the rancher must have expended upon this banquet. But it helped them to understand how he could have offered as the prize for the shooting contest the glorious El Capitán.

Duds Kobbe had adapted himself with the most perfect ease to the big range saddle that was on the back of El Capitán, and which the generosity of Alvarez made a part of the prize. He passed deeper into the domains of Alvarez. He crossed, in the first place, a long drift of rolling hills, covered with rich grass, and now dotted with fat cattle. Then he went on to a valley that was under close cultivation with the plow. It was soil rich enough for truck farming. Vegetables, berries, fruits, were produced in vast bulk from that valley. And this was only a simple unit in the estate. He rode on into an upland district that was a sort of plateau whose level top afforded thousands of acres for the raising of wheat, barley, oats, and hay. From the plateau rose a range of high hills, covered with sturdy pine forests. And these were regularly planted and cut, as he could see in passing through. Beyond this was another huge domain of cow country, all good range. And past the extremity of this district he arrived at the lofty trees, the sweeping lawns where a thousand sprinklers were whirring, and the white walls and the red roofs of the house of Alvarez itself.

But what Duds had seen in his approach had been merely an outer segment, a mere wedge of the whole estate. It swept away on all hands in a great circle. No doubt there were far richer things than any he had seen. In the upper hills—or mountains they might be called—he understood that there were rich copper mines. These, too, were part of the property of Alvarez, and with the lumber, the fruits, the cattle, the horses, the minerals, he could understand how a single horse and a single saddle might not seem too rich a prize for a shooting contest. For the wealth of Alvarez was a thing that he himself no doubt did not understand and perhaps he could not have guessed half its extent.

There was something inspiring in the thought of such money, for it made of Alvarez a king among men in wealth and power. Every man who passed through a corner of the estate of the rich Spanish-American could not help but feel his spirit expand at the thought of possibly rivaling *Don* Ramon.

Kobbe came to the patio and there reined the stallion, for the gates in front of the garden were secured. He looked through the bars at the wide façade and the ponderous overhanging eaves and the great, nobly proportioned windows of the house. It had the simplicity of a true Spanish house of the Southwest, but it had the dignity of an Athenian temple. Duds Kobbe, though he was not easily impressed, gaped like a child at the big building. Presently he found that a dark-skinned servant was grinning at him, nearby. And Kobbe grinned back at him. "Very big," Kobbe said frankly. "Very old?" He asked this in good faith.

The servant shrugged his shoulders. "Five years," he said at last.

"Then *Señor* Alvarez built it?" asked Kobbe with manifest surprise.

"No. It was built by another man."

"Who?"

"I forget. He died afterward. He owed the *señor* money, and so the *señor* took the house."

"Ah," Duds said softly. "I thought it would be something like that. Will you tell him that I am here? He has sent for me."

"What name?" asked the servant.

"Kobbe," said Duds.

And the servant went to execute the order.

IV

The *mozo* returned almost at once and opened the gate, bringing a companion with him who took charge of El Capitán. Then he led Duds Kobbe into the house to Alvarez. The latter was seated in a little study whose walls were lined with books—books that were decorative rather than for use. They were all in extensive sets of green and red and yellow leather, decorated with expensive tooling in gold. And Kobbe could tell at a glance that their set and ordered ranks were not broken by the hands of casual readers. As for the volume that lay on the table near the hand of Alvarez, it was placed there for effect to complete the picture. Kobbe knew all this the instant he stepped through the door. And he knew, furthermore, that he was seated facing the window, while the master of the house had his back to it so that the latter could study him more carefully while his own face remained in the shadow.

"You are kind," said Alvarez, "in coming to me so quickly."

"I hoped to see you at the barbecue," said Kobbe.

"I am not well," said Alvarez. "The doctors have me on a short rein, and I cannot follow my own wishes. Otherwise I should be down there now. But I was long enough at the grounds to see you shoot, *señor*, and to admire you for your skill."

"My horse gave me an easy seat . . . that's the answer," Kobbe said smilingly. "But what is your need of me, *Señor* Alvarez?"

"My need?"

"You have not organized such a festival for nothing."

"Of course not. I have told everyone that my purpose is to begin a long series of such contests. Cool heads and steady hands and straight eyes are worth a great deal, *señor*, and I hope that my little festival will make men value them every year more and more."

"Of course that is one purpose, and a very generous one," replied Kobbe. "But there is another reason. There is a reason that has to do with you, *Señor* Alvarez."

The latter shrugged his shoulders. "I cannot understand," he said.

"If you had given cash prizes, I should not doubt you, but when you give El Capitán . . ."

"After all, a fine horse is only money in another form."

"You made a long trip to England to buy him. He is of great value to you."

"But here he is hardly used for work. He needs to be on the plain and through the mountains with

193

a good rider like yourself, *señor*. I made him one of the prizes for that reason."

"I shall believe that if you wish."

"You speak strangely, *señor*."

"And you, *Señor* Alvarez, act very strangely."

The rancher flushed. "In what way?"

"You have placed men to watch me even while I am talking to you."

"Certainly not!"

"A touch of wind moved a branch of that tree outside the window. It showed me a fellow crouched in the forking of the limbs. He can peer through the leaves and watch everything that passes in the room. And he had a short rifle in his hands so that if he sees a game worth bringing down . . . you understand me, *señor*?"

Alvarez bit his lip and grew even a brighter red. He seemed to hesitate for an instant whether to deny or admit that his guest had seen the truth. "You are very frank," he said at last.

"I must be," answered Duds Kobbe. "If I am to be of use to you and you to me, we must be frank. Must we not?"

"Then tell me your opinion. What do you see that is a mystery? What do you understand my motives to be?"

"In holding the rodeo?"

"Yes."

"The rodeo is a mask. What you wanted was

the shooting contest only. But it would seem too strange if you sent out invitations for that alone. So you arranged a whole rodeo of which the shooting was only a single part."

"You are very sure?"

"I am."

"And what could my purpose have been?"

"To find a fast and accurate shot."

"*Señor*, you grow omnipotent."

"I am sorry if I am wrong."

"Why should I need a fast and accurate shot?"

"To take care of you, *Señor* Alvarez, in place of the doctors."

"What manner of foolish talk is this?"

"Only the truth."

"Do you mean that I wish a gunfighter to cure me of sickness?"

"Of the sort of sickness that troubles you a gunfighter could take much better care than a doctor."

"And what is my ailment, *señor*?"

Duds Kobbe glanced hastily around the room to assure himself they were alone. Then he leaned a little toward his companion so that he could bridge the distance between them with the softest of voices. "Your sickness is called acute fear of sudden death, *Señor* Alvarez."

The rich man half started from his chair. For a moment he remained with his eyes staring, his lips parted, his face the picture of amazement, and his right hand raised in a singular arrested gesture.

"Do not give the signal," said Kobbe, "for if you do, that fellow in the tree will start shooting at me. And if he does, I shall have to try my hand at you."

Alvarez recovered himself with a gasp and sank back. "What under the blue heaven has put this idea into your head?"

"A number of things."

"Name a few, then."

"The first sight of El Capitán. A man does not give up such a horse unless he is in fear of something no less than death."

"This is only an opinion you are giving me, not a fact."

"Well, then, for the facts. I come out here and am brought before the master of the house. I find him reported to be an invalid, hardly able to journey to the field of the rodeo. I come to his house and find him a sturdy-looking man with a fine, clear color . . ."

"There are maladies which do not show in the face, my friend," said Alvarez calmly.

"But if you are not sick, what then is wrong with you? Fear can be like a disease, I have been told. Suppose that fear has kept you in your house, since the attempt was made on your life."

"If I considered myself in danger, there are

capable sheriffs in this country. They would take charge of my problem."

"Suppose that the power you fear is something that a sheriff cannot help. As for sheriffs and men with guns, you could fill your house with them. There is the fellow in the tree outside the window, for instance."

"The blockhead!" exclaimed Alvarez. "He is a pig without sense!"

"He had not counted on the wind. That is all."

"But in short, my plan in holding the rodeo was to secure the most capable bodyguard that I could find, and, in order to do that, I would spare no expense and would use even my finest horse as a bait . . . a horse that my daughter loves passionately . . . yet I give him up as the bait to draw the best man into my trap?"

"That," Kobbe said, "is exactly my idea. Am I wrong?"

The other hesitated a moment, drumming on the arm of his chair and looking straight before him as though, for a moment, he had forgotten about the presence of his guest.

"You are entirely right," he said at last. "I am living in fear of sudden death. I have been existing through this past week in the fear of a knife in the back or a bullet through the heart. And the law I cannot call into my use. How can I tell that the men of the law themselves will not be bribed?"

"How can you tell that I may not be bribed?" asked Kobbe.

"By your face," said Alvarez. "There are certain things that we know by instinct. I think that this is one thing. We know a man as we know a note of music from all other notes. The difference appears to the ear alone and cannot be described. In that way I know that you are an honest man."

"And you know nothing of me except what you have seen?"

"I am not a fool. Do you think that I would put my head into the mouth of a strange lion? I know a great deal more about you than you will imagine. The instant the rodeo began, I started inquiries about every one of the men who were entered for the shooting contest. About you I learned that you were born in Wyoming, were taken East when your uncle with whom you were living . . . because your father had been dead for ten years . . . struck it rich in the mines. That you were educated in the East, but that when your uncle lost his money, you returned to the West again."

"Then," Kobbe said, "you know my father's name?"

"Of course. His name was John Turner. And your name is John Kobbe Turner."

Kobbe, or Turner, as he had just been called, sat stiffly in his chair. Some of the color had left his cheeks. And his eyes had grown as grave and as brilliant as the eyes of a great beast of prey. Alvarez winced before that stare, but he maintained a steady smile as well as he could.

"What more do you know about me?" Kobbe asked.

"That you are a straight shot," said Alvarez. "And that is all I wish to know."

"What is your proposition?" asked Kobbe.

"A salary that you can name at your own pleasure. You will have a room next to my room. It will be your duty to live night and day with weapons at hand ready to come to my help at my first signal. I shall have other guards working outside the house, but if peril comes from within, then I shall have you to strike for me. What do you say to this, *Señor* Turner?"

"Kobbe, if you please."

"By all means, *Señor* Kobbe."

"Give me a moment to think it over."

"As long as you wish."

Kobbe, as he preferred to be called, stood up and walked slowly back and forth across the little room and finally stood in front of the window, looking out upon the garden and the tree that stood in it, holding the guard. He was seeing nothing but his own thoughts, however, and these brought a black frown to his forehead until, out of a side path, a girl walked into his view, singing. She had pushed a small red rose into her black hair. Her face was tilted up by her song and her olive cheeks were bright. Slowly she crossed that part of the garden that Kobbe could overlook, until the weight of his eyes seemed to warn her. She paused suddenly, glanced across to him, and with an exclamation of alarm fled from his view.

He turned slowly to Alvarez. "I shall stay," he said.

V

The stipulations of Alvarez were strict. Kobbe, so long as he cared to stay on the place and with the work, must never leave the immediate precincts of the house and the gardens. He must be ready at any time to accompany Alvarez on journeys, no matter of what extent, and he must hold himself ready, day and night, to come to the defense of the older man with all his skill and with unfailing courage. In return, he was to receive a handsome salary, a chair at the table of Alvarez, a *mozo* to look after his needs, and every possible liberty of motion within the house and its immediate grounds. It was not necessary that he be constantly near the person of Alvarez. It was, however, vital that he be within calling distance at all times.

Kobbe accepted, making only one exception—which was that he be allowed to take one hour's freedom with El Capitán before his period of service began. And so, a few minutes later, he was galloping across the hills at a round rate, with the big chestnut stretching away with a stride as easy as flowing water and almost as smooth.

Kobbe held straight on until he came to a thicket between two hills. There he paused and raised a sharp whistle. It was answered almost at once, and after a moment a second horseman broke out from the covert and rode hastily down to meet him.

The newcomer was a stately fellow, well past middle age, arrow straight in the saddle, with a dark skin and a black eye and a sort of foreign gentility that was as easily distinguishable as the color of his eyes, but which was difficult to describe. He greeted Kobbe by raising his hand in salutation.

"Something has gone wrong, my son," he said as he drew close and reined his horse to a halt.

"It has," said Kobbe.

"What is it?"

"I can't raise a hand against him."

"You?"

"I've made up my mind. I cannot attempt to injure him."

A flush of hot anger settled in the face of the older man, but, like a person of experience, he did not speak for an instant, allowing the flush to subside a little and some of the sparkle to pass out of his eyes.

"What has happened?" he asked at length.

"In the first place, he trusted me."

"And so, in the old days, did we trust him."

"*Señor* Lopez, his crime was committed a long time ago."

"But it has never been forgotten."

"Perhaps you are wrong to keep it so close to your heart all these years."

"Your father would not have been of that opinion."

"You cannot judge. My father was a man who often changed his mind. I remember it very well."

"He could change his mind, but he could never change it about his murderer."

"Murderer? I cannot help thinking that that word is too strong."

"Dastardly murder, John, of a man who trusted him and to whom he owed a great deal."

"Nothing has ever been known for certain."

"We have evidence that only a fool could doubt."

"I shall be sorry to have you write me down a fool."

The older man shrugged his shoulders. "I shall try to be very temperate," he said. "I have no desire to anger you, my boy. I know that whatever conclusion you have come to has the gravest reasons behind it. For you are your father's son, after all, and being his son you must have the strongest desire in your heart to avenge him."

"If I were sure that *Don* Ramon were guilty . . ."

"Call him by his true name."

"Why not by the new name? Under the old name I hate him. Under the new name, I have found him gentle, courteous, and willing to trust me."

"So did we all find him until the time for the test came."

"But consider that for ten years he has been living in this country, and he has taught his servants and his neighbors to love him. They all swear by *Don* Ramon."

"So they might have sworn by your father, if he had been alive. But this treacherous hound removed him from the earth."

"It is not proved. Besides . . . is it not possible for men to change, *señor*?"

"Some man can change from good to better, or from bad to worse. But no man can change his essential nature."

"I cannot help doubting the truth of that."

"Other people have doubted it, but it is always proved."

"If there were not such a thing as repentance, why should people be punished and not destroyed? But society believes that men who have committed one fault may not be necessarily all bad. They may change and learn better ways."

"The spots on the leopard will not change, my son."

"What evil has he done for ten years?"

"He has grown fat with money that is not his. It is easy to be a giver of charity when one is passing on stolen money."

"He has a straight, clear eye, and he talks like a man."

"But he has the heart of a devil under that eye, my young friend. What will the ghost of your murdered father think when he looks down and sees that you are reconciled to his murderer?"

"He will think that I am doing only what my conscience tells me to do."

"Conscience, John?"

"What else?"

"Has the money of Ramon, as you call him, nothing to do with it?"

"Sir?" Kobbe said coldly.

"I am not accusing you. I am only asking you to open your eyes to motives that you yourself may not be aware of."

"His money has no weight with me."

"You are a remarkable young man, then."

"Your tongue is sharp today, señor."

"What has happened? This morning you called him a snake, that should be treated as a snake is treated. How has he changed in the meantime?"

"He has changed by being known."

"John, you are talking lightly to me. Do I deserve no better than this from you?"

"I am talking to you as honestly as I know how."

"Tell me this, then. What do you intend to do?"

"I have taken a new position." He raised his head and looked Lopez firmly in the eye, and yet he flushed in spite of himself, in shame for the thoughts that he knew would spring into the

205

mind of his companion when what he had done was known.

"And that position?" asked Lopez, turning pale.

"You have already guessed it."

"I pray to heaven that I have not guessed correctly."

"Very well, then. I'll tell you in so many words. I already know the way in which you will judge me. I only ask you to keep the spoken words to yourself. Yes, I have taken a position as the bodyguard of *Don* Ramon."

There was a groan from Lopez. "Treason!" he cried at last.

"No, but a love of fair play," Kobbe said.

"Is it fair play to leave us and be bought up by the money that our enemy has stolen from us?"

"I know this much," said Kobbe slowly, making a great effort to control himself, "that *Don* Ramon was always accused by you of having committed a crime that is too detestable to name. Perhaps he is guilty. But my personal feeling, after meeting him face to face and talking with him in his own house, is that he cannot be guilty of such a crime. If I am wrong, I am very sorry."

"You have not only made up your mind that he is innocent, but you have determined to fight for him?"

"There is no one else in the world who *could* fight on his side. There is no one else who knows the names and the faces of the men who are against him. There is no one else who can tell that he is being hounded down by a conspiracy."

"Conspiracy?"

"There is hardly a better word for it. You have tried him according to your own prejudices and not according to the law. You are going to butcher him like a dog if you can. I tell you, *Señor* Lopez, it is going to be my work to keep you from it."

The eyes of the other flashed fire, and his lips worked for a moment before he could speak in answer. "Go back to him, then," he said at last. "Tell him the names, describe our faces, tell him our purpose. He will have the hills combed with posses before midnight has come. He will hunt us down, perhaps. And rather than be caught, we will die fighting, be assured. Our blood will be upon your head. Farewell!"

"Wait," Kobbe said, greatly moved. "You have misunderstood me. I shall not whisper a word that will identify or accuse a single one of you. He already knows something. He knows that there is a conspiracy against him. He knows that I am my father's son. And yet he seems to feel that I cannot be one of the plot to stab him in the darkness. It is going to be my purpose to make him know that he has not been wrong in trusting me, but, at the same time, I had rather have my hands cut off than to speak a word against you. Will you try to believe that?"

"How can I believe that you are able to feel for both sides in a fight?"

"You must believe me, nevertheless."

"Yet you will be with him in his house and you have sworn that if he is attacked you will defend him."

"I have."

"Do you see what that means, John?"

"In what way?"

"It means that you, being our enemy, we must protect ourselves from your interference."

"And that?"

"John, we have sworn to stay together until we have destroyed our enemy. If we find an obstacle in our path, even if it is the son of the man we loved most in the world, do you think that we can afford to hesitate, knowing that we will be truer to his memory and to his wishes than you?"

"You will try to get rid of me, then?"

"If you stay with him, we must, John, if you feel that we are wrong, stand aside and take no part on either side. I tell you, you cannot save him except by betraying us to the law. And if you try to foil us with your single hand, you only bring destruction on your own head as well as upon his. Do you understand me?"

"I wish that I had never heard you speak as you have just done."

"It is the truth."

"Then go back and tell the others that I have made up my mind."

"What shall I tell them?"

"That I am staying with *Don* Ramon, and that, if he is attacked, I shall shoot to kill in his defense."

"God forgive you, John."

"And may God forgive you, *Señor* Lopez. But I swear to you that, if you yourself come near *Don* Ramon, I shall shoot you through the body if my gun is out before yours."

"And I swear to you, John, that your death is not twenty-four hours away!"

They reined back their horses until a considerable distance lay between them. Then Kobbe twisted his mount around and sent the chestnut flying down the hollow.

VI

But the words of Lopez were working most effectually when Kobbe was far out of his sight, for he turned back and forth through his mind what his late companion had said and he began to confess to himself that it was not a true faith in the honesty of Alvarez that kept him with the latter. It was because he had caught one glimpse of the girl who walked through the garden, and he knew that if he left the service of *Don* Ramon, he was also leaving behind all hope of ever seeing her again. And see her again he must, for in that instant she had been stamped into his soul. She had added something to his life. It seemed to Kobbe that he was no longer the man he had been before that vision in the garden. He was happier, he was far stronger. How else could he have faced Lopez without being overawed by that solemn gentleman?

Yet, knowing guiltily that it was for the sake of the girl that he had denied the arguments of Lopez, he could not feel any great repentance. All shadows disappeared in the glorious thought that he was soon to meet her at the dinner table.

He was back at the house so late that he had barely time to get ready for the evening meal, and when he went into the library, he found the girl and *Don* Ramon already there and waiting.

She was presented to him as *Señorita* Mantiez. It was a great surprise to Kobbe, but he made up his mind that she must be a protégée of the rich man—perhaps his niece, perhaps the daughter of some unfortunate friend who had died. But he had no energy left for the determination of her place in the household. All his wits were occupied in the task of watching her with consummate attention and at the same time screening that examination from the eyes of *Don* Ramon.

The *señorita* wore a dress of yellow lace—it was closer to ivory than to yellow. And she wore no ornament whatever, saving a single ring with a single ruby set in it. It was a marvelous stone, and Kobbe wondered why women ever wore more than one jewel, and that a ruby. Sometimes it sent an arrow of crimson through the water glass. Sometimes it flashed near the face of the girl and made her seem pale and her eyes great and dark and tragically dull. And again its flash sparkled with the chime of her laughter. And again, it was a bright touch of fire that gave brilliance to her gesture.

And she made so lovely a picture as she chatted with them that Kobbe could hardly answer her when she spoke to him. He could only pray that his silence would be taken as absent-mindedness or as dullness of wit. Anything was preferable to their knowledge that he was lost in the worship of her beauty.

Her first name was Miriam, and the mere turning of that name through his mind enchanted Kobbe. Miriam Mantiez! It seemed to him that there was soft mystery and exquisite charm in that phrase. And he repeated it gently to himself.

The rancher had said: "You must not trouble *Señor* Kobbe with talk, Miriam. He is busy with his thoughts. And one of those thoughts may be worth a very great deal to me. Who knows what he has discovered or what he has seen or where he has been in that ride that he took just before dinner?"

There was a very patent query behind this placid question. But Kobbe returned no answer.

"Unless," continued Alvarez, chuckling, "he was considering the question of the man in the tree. You see," he added, "that Miriam knows all my thoughts, all my plans, all my past, all my future, all my hopes. And you may talk with perfect freedom before her."

Kobbe murmured that this was interesting, but that his ride had showed him nothing of importance.

"Except a look at the landscape?" queried the rancher.

"Yes," said Kobbe.

"And no one else?"

It was a very sharp touch and Kobbe straightened a little under the prick of it. "What do you mean, *Señor* Alvarez?"

"Nothing," the rancher said, smiling broadly. "But there are people as well as trees growing on my estate, you know."

It was plain that he had been informed of the interview between Kobbe and Lopez. No doubt he had been told the name of the other, that one of his men had watched the meeting from a distance. And the connotation of this was that Alvarez was keeping spies upon the trail of Kobbe every moment of his stay on the place. Yet when Kobbe met the eyes of Alvarez steadily, the latter turned his glance away, and it was plain that he was not suspicious about the results of the conversation. It was almost as though his spy had heard the exact words of the talk between him and Lopez. And Kobbe could not keep a slight flush from his face. At the same time he felt two things about Alvarez. The one was that the rich *don* was as full of craft as a serpent. The other was that the complacent laughter of Alvarez showed that he was certain that Kobbe was entirely pledged to his service. And one conclusion was as disagreeable as the other to Kobbe.

Dinner ended. They settled down in a high-vaulted music room and Miriam played for them at a piano and then sang. In the pauses, the beat and faint humming of a distant banjo kept breaking in from far away by the servants' quarters beyond the house. Kobbe moved closer to the window until he could look out, and he saw two men pacing ceaselessly up and down on the inside of the wall of hewn rock. They carried rifles, and their whole manner was that of soldiers. No doubt there were other men armed in this fashion and in this fashion mounting guard over the house of the rich man. Was it not strange, then, that Alvarez should pay so much money and so much attention in order to secure one more guard on the inside of the house? He resolved to put that question to the master of the house at the first opportunity. Or was it not better to leave well enough alone? What he desired was to stay near this charming girl until—he hardly knew what.

A servant entered with a whispered message for Alvarez. He rose at once and left the room after an apology to *Señorita* Mantiez, and a wave to Kobbe. Kobbe half expected that she would turn to him and begin a conversation of some sort. And in fact, as her fingers trailed carelessly through some meaningless chords, he thought that she was about to end and was merely hunting for an opening word to begin the talk. He decided to help her.

"May I take that chair at your right?" asked Kobbe.

"Stay where you are," she said.

He could hardly believe his ears. "I didn't quite hear you," said Kobbe.

"Stay where you are," she said, and began to play something that he did not recognize, just loud enough, as it seemed to him, to enable her to speak to him without fearing that the sound of her voice would carry any farther than his ear. And the heart of Kobbe began to race.

"Do you mean . . . ?"

"That he is still watching, of course."

Kobbe flushed and set his teeth. "You must smoke and look happy," she said.

Automatically he produced a cigarette. "Because of what? Of *Señor* Alvarez?"

"Yes. He is very suspicious, and he can almost read minds, *Señor* Kobbe, when he is excited."

"That's not very amiable."

"Not at all."

"Why does he do it?"

"He is jealous."

"Jealous?" Kobbe stared at her.

"That is it. He is afraid of other men . . . because he is older than I, you see?"

He would have paid a year of life for the sake of seeing her face as she talked. "Do you mean to say . . . I cannot understand you, *señorita*."

"We are betrothed, *señor*. I am surprised that he did not tell you."

"Not a word. But . . . you will be a very great

lady as the wife of *Señor* Alvarez. I wish you great happiness, also."

"I shall be happy enough, thank you. But people do not marry for romance in these times, of course."

"They do not?"

"No. Girls must realize that life is a hard business proposition."

"Ah?"

"And so they are raised to look for contentment in marriage . . . not great happiness. *Señor* Alvarez has explained it all to me many times."

Kobbe could not speak. He puffed at the cigarette until he had regained his composure. He managed to say at last: "It is all a new theory to me."

"Oh, it is not a theory. It is a fact."

"He is very sure."

"He knows the facts."

"What are they, please?"

"When people are driven along by a great, wild love, they are wildly happy for a month, and then they begin to be discontented. Then they grow unhappy. Then they regret. Then they begin to hate each other."

"You speak like a professor of love, *señorita*."

"Oh, no. Only what he has taught me. But the reason is that love is blind, you know."

"I have read that in a book, I think."

"It simply means that when people are in

love, they are not seeing one another, for they are merely seeing their love. But when the love grows just a little cold, then they begin to see the truth. And it is always such a great way below the thing they saw in their blindness that they can hardly stand the shock of that truth."

"Do none stand it successfully?"

"Almost none," she said.

"Except one's own parents," he said.

"Mine died while I was only a baby," she said. "And yours?"

"They worshiped each other."

"And did they begin with true love?"

"Like music," he said. "He was coming down from a mine where he had been working. His hands were sore, his legs were tired, his pockets were empty. His winter's work had been for nothing, and he had his jaw set for fighting. Then he saw my mother galloping her horse across the trail, with a white feather in her hat, and the wind rippling in her hair. He saw her, and he loved her. They were married in a week. And they loved each other to the day of their deaths."

"Is it true?" she said. And her fingers ceased upon the piano.

"Perfectly true."

Then she began to play very softly on the piano, drawling the phrases of the music, and all of them were filled with a speaking sadness.

"I wish," she said at last, "that you had not told me that."

"Why?"

"Because I think that I should have been happier without knowing."

And Kobbe knew that his words had taken hold upon her and were working deep and deeper into her mind.

VII

She was thrumming at the piano again, but the music was so soft that he knew it could not interrupt her thoughts.

"Oh, of course," she said at last, "I understand that there are these romances. But most of them are in books. However, *Señor* Alvarez and I have decided that the other way is the safer way."

"You and *Señor* Alvarez?" he echoed as the picture grew bright in his mind.

"I'm surprised that he hasn't told you, since he knows that you're to be with us for such a long time." Still she played the piano. Still her head was turned from him.

He came to his feet, and at the noise she turned toward him. It was only for a glance, but he could tell in that instant that at the least she was not happy. And he forgot that he was showing her the misery of his own face. This child, with all the beauty of her life before her, to be wedded to a man past the middle of his life, gray, already half prepared for the grave.

He murmured something as an excuse and stumbled out of the room, out of the house. In the garden he dropped on a bench and turned his face up to the stars and the cool of the wind. But when he was motionless, his torment grew too great for him to bear. He started up and began to pace back and forth, for when he was in motion, he could struggle better toward a solution of his problem.

She was to marry Alvarez. For that purpose doubtless he had raised her, reveling in the prospect of her beauty one day becoming his. She had passed from his protégée to his fiancée, and in the end she was to be his wife. That certainly must be the story. He saw the tall form of a guard stalking near the wall, and accosted him, for the fellow might be able to tell him something worth knowing.

He had expected a Spanish accent, for in New Mexico Spanish is far more familiar than English, and particularly on the estate of a Spanish-American.

"Maybe you're Kobbe?" he said.

"That's my name."

"Well," said the guard, "darned if I ain't glad to see you. I guess you're here on the same business that keeps me."

"Perhaps. What's your work?"

"Chasing around . . . hunting ghosts."

"Ghosts?"

"Ever since that gent shoved a knife at Alvarez he's been scared green. I'm to keep guard here like a soldier. If I see anybody sneaking around, I'm to holler to 'em once, and then start shooting."

"Maybe the fellow Alvarez shot is one of a

220

gang. Maybe Alvarez is waiting for the next one of the gang to show up?"

"Did he tell you that?" murmured the guard. "He's dreaming, partner. I've lived around these parts a mighty long time before Alvarez come, and I've been here all the time that Alvarez has been here. He ain't made no enemies. He's a sure enough quiet one. Besides, the folks in this neighborhood ain't the kind that gang together to get a man. They do their hunting one by one."

"Perhaps it's all in the imagination of *Señor* Alvarez."

"It sure is. By the way, I was over to see the shooting today. That was neat work you done. When I seen you knock them cans over I says to myself . . . 'Alvarez will want Kobbe to help on this job.' And by Jiminy, here you are." He laughed softly, rocking back and forth. "You'll get easy work and fat pay," he said. "I guess me and Harry, yonder, and the others, do the outside work, and you work on the inside. All I got to say is that if anybody tries to do anything to Alvarez, he's going to get filled with lead."

"What does Miss Mantiez think?" asked Kobbe.

"She don't do no thinking except what Alvarez tells her to do," said the cowpuncher sourly.

"How can that be?"

"Why, since her dad died . . ."

"Who was he?"

221

"I see you're a sure enough stranger around here."

"I am."

"Well, Mantiez used to own this here ranch. He was a fine old gent. He was always giving a show of some kind or other. Gave so many that everybody called this Rodeo Ranch. Gave so many that he got plumb in debt. He was sort of everybody's friend. Couldn't say no to a stranger, even. If a miner was broke, he'd come in to *Señor* Mantiez. If a cowpuncher was down on his luck, he could get a job or a stake or leave to lie around and get chuck with the other boys until he was fed up fat or landed a job somewhere. That was the sort that Mantiez was.

"Of course he'd run over his head in debt. Everybody owed him, and he owed the bank. Finally along comes Alvarez, buys in on the bank, and decides that he wants this ranch. He closes in on the ranch, Mantiez has to lay down, and inside of a month the ranch belonged to Alvarez and Mantiez had died of something or other . . . I dunno what. Everybody said that it was a busted heart that really killed him. He had to trust everybody, of course. The last person he trusted was Alvarez. He turned over his girl to him. And dog-gone me if he didn't do a good job of it."

"Made Alvarez guardian of the girl?"

"Right. And Alvarez has been working ever

since for her. Gave her a dog-gone' fine education. Had all kinds of teachers here for her and . . ."

"But never sent her away to school?"

"Sure, he didn't. He kept her here and spent five times as much as it would cost if she'd gone to a school, everybody says. And now, what d'you think?"

"Well?"

"As if he hadn't done enough for her already, Alvarez is going to up and marry her." He shook his head in wonder at such greatness of heart.

"He's a lucky man," Kobbe said.

"Lucky? Giving her this here whole ranch? Why, he ain't got any other heir. It'll all go to that girl."

"Do you think that had any weight with her?"

"She's human, I guess," said the other. "But the main thing was that she don't know how to think anything different from what Alvarez tells her. However, everybody agrees that it's pretty fine of Alvarez to turn this here ranch back to the Mantiez family. But about that El Capitán horse . . . "

Kobbe hardly heard the question. He returned a vague answer and strolled off through the garden. He passed down the side of the house and to the rear, out of sight of the guard, and it was when he approached the broad shining face of a pool into which the fountain had ceased playing that the shot was fired. The wasp hum darted past his

223

forehead, but he was already in mid-air, leaning back into the shrubbery near the pool.

Another bullet followed him and clipped a slender branch above his head and sent it rustling down. Then Kobbe went into action. He had seemed formidable enough in the broad light of the day at the rodeo. But here under the starlight he was turned into a great lurking cat. Behind him he could hear the distant shout of the guard. But he did not wait for assistance. He raced through the shrubbery and darted straight at the wall of the garden.

From behind it he saw the head and shoulders of a man and a gun raised. At the flash of metal he fired, heard a muffled cry, and the figure disappeared. In another instant he was on top of the wall. He saw just beneath him—for a declivity of the ground beyond the wall made it considerably lower than the garden side—a horse with an empty saddle, and, on the ground beside the horse, a motionless form.

He dropped down, kicked the revolver away from the hand of the fallen man, and jerked the limp figure to its knees. Then he found that he was looking into the face of Lopez! He swore softly beneath his breath, and Lopez groaned a response.

Kobbe released his grip, and the other staggered to his feet. For a second he groped idly around him as though to make sure of his surroundings or to reach his fallen weapon. Then his senses seemed to return. He drew himself up and glared at Kobbe.

"In the name of heaven, Lopez," Kobbe said, "have you descended to this? Are you hunting me as if I were a rat?"

Lopez supported his right arm with his left. It was plain that the bullet had struck the gun, cast it into the face of Lopez with stunning force, and had then glanced away from the metal and ripped up the arm of Lopez.

"I hunted you like a rat," Lopez said, "because whatever you may be to other men, to us you are only a traitor."

"Get on your horse," Kobbe responded. "And you're lucky that your traitor does not treat you according to your own fashion."

"You let me go at your own peril," answered Lopez. "For if I escape now, I shall come again, John, until we have wiped you out of the way. Alvarez is doomed."

"I take the peril," Kobbe answered hastily. "Now get into the saddle. They're coming. If they see us together, I'll be compelled to take you in spite of myself."

Lopez hesitated. But whatever was in his mind remained unspoken. He turned, caught the horn of the saddle with his unwounded arm, and dragged himself up. A touch of his spurs sent him flying over the slope, while a shout from the wall warned Kobbe that the guard had come up at last.

Kobbe jerked up his revolver and opened a fire that was intentionally wild. From the wall the guard was alternately shooting and cursing, but Lopez, leaning low over the neck of a fast horse, was almost instantly screened by a veil of mist.

VIII

There was a wild pursuit. Kobbe himself was in the van on the chestnut, but, in spite of the speed of the stallion, Lopez had gained a lead that could not be overcome, nor could his trail be followed. They came back late in the night and Kobbe found that a message was waiting for him to come at once to Alvarez. He found the rancher walking in deep thought up and down the library. It was not hard to see that he was very excited and very angry.

When Kobbe entered, he was given hardly a glance by his employer, who strode over to the fireplace and, with his hands clasped behind his back and his back turned to Kobbe, puffed viciously at a cigar and snapped his words over his shoulder. "What luck this evening, Kobbe?"

"He had too long a start," said Kobbe. "We had no luck at all."

"Your horse was not fast enough?"

"I had to keep back with the others. My speed was their speed."

"What made you stay with them?"

"I might have run into a trap if I had gone on by myself."

"You are paid to take chances, Kobbe."

"I am not paid to throw my life away."

"Good!" But the snarl with which he spoke meant quite the opposite of the word. "When Jenkins found you, what were you doing?"

"Trying to drop him with a chance shot."

"But again you had no luck?"

"None."

"Today, when your horse was galloping, you shot tin cans from the top of posts a dozen or twenty feet away."

"Well?"

"This evening, when you were not in the saddle, you miss shots at a man and a horse not five paces off?"

"There is a difference between day and night."

"Very true. But the stars are bright."

"Besides, there is a difference between shooting at a target, even at a very small one, and at a man, even a big one. If that were not true, in the old days the good shots would always have won the duels."

"Kobbe, who was the man?"

"The man? I have not the slightest idea."

"What had happened before?"

"He shot at me from behind the garden wall, while I was walking down by the pool. I jumped over the fence and . . ."

"You ran straight at him?"

"Through the brush and then at the wall from the side so that I took him by surprise. He shot at me and I at him. He fell and I jumped over the fence after him."

"Ah?"

"I saw him lying flat. I called out to him to surrender. Instead, he caught up his revolver and threw it at me. It was a lucky aim. The gun hit my arm and made me drop my revolver, which fell several steps away. I ran to scoop it up, but by that time he was in the saddle and riding away and Jenkins was shooting at him over the wall."

"You let a wounded man get away from you?" Alvarez whirled upon him. "Do you think I would be wise to allow such an unlucky man to work for me?"

The first answer that jumped to the lips of Kobbe was a careless and impertinent reply, but he knew that if he angered Alvarez, it meant that he had seen the girl for the last time. And that would be a disaster. He could not get out of his head the picture of her as she had turned toward him from the piano, curious, sad, searching eyes. He must see her at least once more and determine if she were truly happy in the thought of her approaching marriage.

"You have been guarded by a number of men for a whole week," he said.

"What has that to do with it?"

"How many men have they even touched with a bullet?" asked Kobbe.

"But perhaps they have no enemies?"

"Do you think it was my enemy who fired at me when I was in the garden?"

"Why not? They could never mistake you for me."

"They may wish to get me out of the way before they attempt to get at you."

Talk had relieved the anger of Alvarez somewhat. Now he broke suddenly into laughter. "Well," he said, "the main thing is that you made the rascal run, and that you nipped him with a bullet . . . a rather bad wound, too, for I myself searched the place and saw the stains in the grass. But, Kobbe, I'm very curious to know what it was that you talked about with him."

"Talked about? Nothing."

The rancher began to nod, looking half in anger and half in whimsical amusement at Kobbe. "Jenkins saw you jump over the fence whole seconds before he came up. But when he arrived, you still had not had time to finish your enemy. Kobbe, be frank with me."

"I am frank as I can be."

"You will not tell me who he was?"

"I do not know."

"Suppose what he said to you was . . . 'Alvarez can only be willing to pay you a few hundreds for his life. But we will pay you as many thousands for his death.' Suppose that he said only those few words to you."

230

Kobbe shrugged his shoulders and allowed the other to study him at leisure.

"Come," said Alvarez suddenly. "I have this to show you." He led his companion to a small desk at the corner of the room. From the upper part of it he jerked out a little drawer that was tightly packed with a whole stack of greenbacks.

"Today," he said, "I was paid an old debt, and I was paid in cash. Count it, Kobbe."

Kobbe flicked over a few bills to catch the denominations. "There are several thousands here," he said.

"There are as many thousands as there are days remaining in this month," he said. "And if I am still alive at the end of this month, the money is yours, Kobbe. Do you understand?"

"That is too generous."

"My friend, if I could be sure that you will put all your heart and your brain into this work of defending me, I'd double and treble that sum. My life is in your hands. I am a fool if I do not treat my life with caution."

"Why do you trust so much in me?" Kobbe asked suddenly.

The rancher made a vague gesture. "If *you* cannot save me," he said, "no one can save me. That much I know." He changed the subject suddenly. "You did not stay long with Miss Mantiez?"

"I did not," admitted Kobbe.

"She thought your leaving was rather strange."

"I am sorry."

"I fear you are not a great man with the ladies, Kobbe."

"I fear I am not," Kobbe concurred. "If you have depended upon me to entertain Miss Mantiez, I shall disappoint you again."

And it was plain that the rancher was delighted.

"If we must get along without your talk," he said, "we must do as best we may do. And if . . ."

Here there was the long and almost human sighing of a draft across the room, and Alvarez whirled as though his name had been called. He saw only a yawning door and the black hall beyond it, yet the sight seemed to steal all his manhood away. He sank into a chair, gasping: "Kobbe . . . for heaven's sake . . . see what it is. Help . . ."

Kobbe ran to the door and looked down the hall. There was nothing there. He closed the door and turned back with that report. "It was only the work of the wind," he said.

"Do you think so?" replied Alvarez sneeringly, some of his courage returning. "Do you think it is only the wind? I tell you, they have surrounded my house and they are *in* my house. Perhaps *you* are one of them. Perhaps they have poisoned the mind of Miriam against me. Perhaps her hand will tomorrow pour a few drops in the wine that will . . ." He broke off with a shudder. And then he added solemnly: "Never think that I am a foolish neurasthenic. I tell you, Kobbe, that there are men in this world who would give their own lives for the sake of taking mine. They have hunted me for years. They have found me at last. The first of them I have killed with my own hand. But the second . . . who knows what will happen when the second sneaks inside my house, unless a brave man like you protects me. Good night. And remember, that when I call from my room after dark . . . if it is only so much as a whisper . . . if it is only a sound that you imagine . . . if it sounds only like the beating of the feet or the hands of a man who is being strangled so that he cannot cry out before his death . . . or if in the middle of the night a mere suspicion stirs in you . . . then, for heaven's sake, jump from your bed, seize your guns, and dash into my room. Do you hear me, Kobbe?" And he clutched the arm of his companion with shaking hands.

Kobbe turned his head a little away from that yellowed face of fear. "I shall do my best," he said.

IX

There was no sleep for Kobbe that night. He undressed, went to bed, and made desperate efforts to concentrate on lines of passing sheep, and on columns of figures, but all sleep-producing devices were of no avail. Finally he dressed again, replaced his guns on his person, and went into the hall. He paced up and down for some time when the door of the room of Alvarez was snatched open and Alvarez himself looked wildly out upon him with a revolver clutched in his hand.

"Praise heaven it is you, Kobbe," Alvarez said. "I listened to that cursed pacing up and down the hall . . . just a whisper and a creak, now and then . . . until it seemed to me that I could count my murderers gathering. I tried to push open the door into your room. I had forgotten that it can only be opened from your side. Finally I determined to rush out and fight for my life. And then I see it is only you . . . walking here deliberately back and forth . . . keeping on the watch to save me. Kobbe, God bless you for it."

Kobbe saw tears glinting on his cheeks. He felt a touch of shame. Certainly it had not been on account of Alvarez that he had conducted that midnight promenade.

"Go down to the main hall," said Alvarez. "If you will stay up this night for my sake, go down to the main hall and watch there. I have dreamed of them for a week slipping in from the rear garden and coming through the hall and up the steps, softly and silently. Go quickly, Kobbe. That is the place to watch tonight. Let the hall be. They will beat down Jenkins and the other guards. They will come in a silent wave through the garden and enter the house."

Of course, to Kobbe, it seemed madness. But he could do nothing but obey. He saw the rancher turn, a bowed, slow-moving figure, into his room, and then Kobbe went to the great hall.

The approach to it was down a short range of steps, for though the building was of one story, it was constructed upon several levels, according to the original disposition of the ground, and the wing of the bedchambers was at a considerable elevation above the great hall and the living rooms. The hall itself extended through the entire breadth of the house, with great French doors opening on the garden of the patio and the garden behind the house. Into it he passed, and, finding a corner chair, he looked over the apartment.

With its lofty ceiling and spacious floor it was worthy in dimensions of some old baronial hall. At parts of it he could only guess, for there was not a light burning. But the moon had lately risen and was pouring its slant light through the tall

235

eastern windows, and that light was dimly caught up by the big mirrors that were built into the walls on all sides, so that the hall was half light and half shadow and even the light parts were little more than starlight darkness.

His mind was still far from his task as guard and deep in the problem of Alvarez and his strange prepossessions when he heard a light whispering sound on the steps that led down from the upper level and into the big room. He had barely time to shrink out of his chair and kneel behind it when a glimmering figure in white stole into view, paused, and then went slowly on in ghostly silence so far as any footfall was concerned, but with the same light whispering of silk against silk.

It crossed the hall and was swallowed in the blackness of an opposite doorway. Kobbe was instantly after her. When he reached the doorway, the figure was gone, but when he hurried on to the next chamber, he saw it again, a pale form disappearing into the music room. From the doorway, he listened to faint music beginning on the piano, touched so very softly that it was like a ghost of sound. And as he listened, it seemed to Kobbe that he recognized some of the same strains that Miriam Mantiez had played that evening while he sat in the room and while they talked cautiously, just above the sound of the strings.

He glided into the room. A great block of moonshine, white as marble, lay upon the floor just beyond the piano. And the room beyond the shaft of light was black with dull outlines—all dull saving for that one form at the piano that seemed to shine by a faint radiance of its own. And he knew that it was Miriam.

The ghostly coldness that had possessed his blood was dissipated. He could suddenly breathe freely. His heart leaped. And when he spoke, he knew what answer he would receive. For she had come down here in the middle of the night to play over again the music that she had played for him that evening. Yes, surely his words to her had sunk far deeper than he had dreamed.

He called softly, and she swerved away from the piano, and the moonlight cascaded over her and made her an exquisite creature of light. She recognized him in the next instant and managed a shaky laugh when he came forward.

"I thought . . . a ghost," she said.

"And I thought the same thing," he said.

"But why are you here?"

"And you," he said, "why are you here?"

"I could not sleep," she said.

"Nor I," Kobbe admitted. "What kept you awake?"

"Oh, I have insomnia now and then."

"I was awake, thinking," said Kobbe.

"Unhappy thoughts, then?"

"Yes, partly. And some very happy ones. I was thinking over all the things that I might have said to you this evening, and which I forgot to say."

"Ah? Then I am glad that I have come down here."

"But I shall never be able to tell them to you."

"And why?"

"They are the sort of things one tells only to oneself."

"I am a kind critic," said Miriam.

And she said it in such a way that he found himself stealing close and closer to her without his own volition. He came so close that he could see her smile.

"If you tempt me to speak, we may both regret it."

There, certainly, was warning enough. But she did not draw back.

"I know," she said. "All the time I have been in my room I have been trying to guess at the things that were just behind the words you were speaking. I have tried to guess. But I cannot guess. That's why I want to hear them now."

"And whatever they are, you'll forgive them?"

"I promise. Because they will be the truth."

"They will be the truth, I think. But do you know the old story of what happened to people on the night of midsummer?"

"Well? They were enchanted with a happy madness."

"That's it, exactly. I am enchanted with a happy madness that makes me say things that I should not say otherwise. But it makes me say that when I met you I became very eager for your happiness. You seemed to me so lovely and so good that I made myself happy imagining the sort of life you were to lead after I saw no more of you. And when I learned afterward that your life was to be spent as the wife of *Señor* Alvarez . . ."

"Hush," she whispered.

"No one can hear me."

"I tell you that the stones of the house have ears for that name."

"I know one thing . . . that you don't worship him blindly, as other people think you do. That he is no oracle to you, as others think."

"How do you know that?"

"I have myself heard you say that he eavesdrops upon you. And in the whole world there's nothing more cowardly and small-souled than that."

"Please . . . please. If you say such things . . ."

"The floor will gape under us and swallow us both. Is that it?"

"I only warn you that we must not think of such things. How I could have said what I did to you, I don't know. But when he left us alone this evening, it seemed to me a trap. Because he knows what is going on in my mind every instant."

"Nonsense. That's just hysteria."

"And yet if you knew all the things I could tell you . . . but when you were in the room and when I was playing for you, I was afraid of what would happen if he read my thoughts."

"And why?"

"Because all at once it came over me . . . choked me . . . a wave of knowledge that I had been hideously lonely all my life and that I should be lonely all my days to come. And that I had missed and would always miss something that you have and that all sunlight people have."

"What can you mean by that?"

"I don't know, except that the life I have led here seems made up of shadows and no substance. Can you understand? I feel as if every day was like the day that went before, and that other days would follow exactly like it. I feel as if I were not real, but just a mirror reflecting a pale image of something that I might be."

"And it was this evening you felt it?"

"Yes."

"When we were talking here?"

"Yes, yes."

"Then," he said, "it *is* magic, but white magic, you know. For I felt the same thing. As if to take you out of this house would be to lead you out of a darkness into the sun."

"Ah, that is it."

"But instead, you are to stay here as the wife of an old man."

"Hush."

"But why under heaven do you do it? This is a free country."

"Nothing that comes near him remains free very long. Everything, sooner or later, becomes afraid of him."

"Do you mean to say . . . ?"

"Oh, yes. Don't you see that what other people think is worship of him . . . is simply terror that freezes my mind and my soul? I dread him more than I dread death."

X

The shock of it numbed Kobbe's very brain. She slipped closer to him, her eyes going wildly over his shoulder on either side, as if searching out an invisible danger that must be gliding upon them. Now she was clinging to him, and her great eyes were fixed upon his.

"Do you know that I have not had the courage to tell you that there is danger threatening you here in this house? Do you know that?"

"Threatening me here? Yes, I think many people know that. From the outside there are . . ."

"Not the outside . . . not the outside. That's not it. I lay awake on my bed trying to puzzle it out. That was after he told me this evening. For he tells me everything, you know. He feels that I am such a part of him that he can tell me everything. He cannot see that I hate and loathe him and all his thoughts. Oh, with all of his brains and his devilishness, he cannot see that I know him and hate what I know. But tonight . . . ah . . . what is that?"

She swayed to one side, but he caught her and supported her, and at the same time, swinging around, he surveyed the doorway with the muzzle of his revolver. It was only an instant, but in that instant she depended upon him for protection, and in that instant joy almost burst his heart. He could have faced lions with his bare hands.

"Praise heaven. But we must not stay here. If he is not here, he is coming."

"We cannot stir until you've told me what the danger is that threatens me."

"Haven't you guessed?"

"No."

"It is he . . . it is Alvarez."

"He?"

"When you came, he told me about it. You are one of his enemies."

"Did he know that? I knew that he might have guessed it because his spies had told him my real name."

"Not his spies. He could recognize you by your face. You are much like your father, he says, and your father was a man who once injured Alvarez."

"Injured him? The lying hypocrite . . ."

"He is worse than that. Only I know what he truly is. But about you . . . he told you that he knew your name. But it was only so that by telling you part of the truth he could keep you from guessing that he understood everything."

"And what is that everything?"

"If he knew that I were telling you, he would have me burned inch by inch."

"He shall never touch you with the weight of a finger."

"Then this is it. He says that you are one of a whole gang. The first man to attack him was a member. And others were to follow, he told me. He was in constant peril of his life. So he determined to get an expert fighter's protection, and he started the rodeo. He said that he knew one of his enemies would appear at that rodeo in the hope that they could get into the house and there murder him. He expected that some enemy whose face was unknown to him . . ."

"And that was I?"

"That was you. When he brought you home, he told me that he had the prize he wanted. He had one of the enemy's camp, and he would buy you. And having bought you, he would have a protector who knew the faces and all the plans of all of his enemies. No one else could be so valuable. Everything was prepared for your coming as if it were a stage."

"He was so sure I'd answer his invitation?"

"Yes. He was sure of that. And once you came here he depended on his money to buy you. But even his money would not do entirely. He said that money was strong, but sometimes romance was stronger, and so he planned it that I should walk in the garden outside the window while he was talking with you. He even told me what dress I should wear so as to make the best possible picture."

"He was right," murmured Kobbe. "It was you

244

who kept me here. But what a dog he is to make you bait."

"I was more ashamed than by anything else he has ever made me do. And when I looked through the window and saw your face and your honest eyes looking out at me . . . I could not stand it. I turned and ran."

"God bless you."

"But now you understand only part. When he has finished using you, he is going to destroy you. He has told me that. And he has no shame or remorse about it. He says that you started to threaten his life and therefore it is only logical and just that he should threaten your life. When you are no longer of advantage to him, he'll wipe you out of his way. He says it is the rule of war. And if he knew now what I have told you, he'd destroy us both, and . . ."

Again fear choked her. He took both her hands.

"Listen to me. He'll do neither of us a harm. We're leaving this house. And we leave together. God help him if he tries to stop us."

"But he has armed men . . ."

"I know his armed men. If I have to shoot my way through them, I'll do it. But it won't come to that. Tell me one thing first . . . why is he so afraid if he knows so much about what is going on among his enemies?"

"Because though he trusts that you will be enough to save him, you expect to become rich

245

from the work, and because you know the plans of your other friends. Because he is as cowardly as he is cruel."

"I believe in the cowardice. I've seen it. Yet tell me, if you fear and hate him so, why have you stayed here?"

"Because I didn't know where to go if I left this place. And I had no one who I could trust to go with me."

"And was that all?"

"A hundred times it has been all that kept me from leaving. A hundred times I have lain awake at night and wondered how God could let me keep living in such unhappiness."

"Does it mean that you will leave this house with me . . . at once . . . tonight?"

"The moment I can get a cloak."

"Do not wait even for that."

"I must."

"And you have thought that if you leave you will become poor at a step?"

"I have thought of that. That is less than nothing."

"Before you go to your room, shall I tell you the true story of how I happened to come hunting Alvarez?"

"I know that there was a good reason."

"It was like this . . . ten years ago my father was in South America. He was rich in coffee plantations, and he had a wide circle of friends who were also great growers. And they, again, were affiliated with other people, and the whole made a large and powerful party in politics. They grew discontented with the harsh treatment that they received from the party that was in power. Finally they were so badly treated that there were imprisonments. And then they decided on a rebellion. In the party that had decided to rebel was my father, and of the others the most prominent was a man named Quinnado. It was Quinnado who first had become discontented with the government. It was Quinnado who first schemed to rebel. It was Quinnado who was the backbone of the whole affair.

"But at the last moment Quinnado disappeared from the country, and at the same moment the chief heads of the proposed rebellion were arrested, given sham trials, and immediately executed. My father was one of those who paid the penalty.

"Of course the reasoning of the other leaders was perfectly simple. It was known that Quinnado had sold his entire estates at a handsome figure, and he had vowed that he would use the entire sum to forward the revolution. This seemed so extremely generous that the other members of the revolutionary party immediately made him treasurer of the scheme and turned into his hands immense sums of money that they had raised for the war that was to come. The size of the sum was too much for Quinnado. He must have sold the secrets of the party to the government for a bonus of hard cash plus liberty to leave the country and go abroad where he could settle down in a new place with a new name, since it was certain that he could never live in his native land where so many hundreds of orphans and infuriated relatives would be willing to sell their own lives if they might take his in exchange.

"That was the general theory. But there were some who felt that Quinnado had been done away with and that his body had been lost as well as the names of those who murdered him.

"Nevertheless, among those of the revolutionists who survived there were some who escaped the proscription and who organized themselves for the purpose of hunting down Quinnado and pinning the result of his crimes upon him, if he were actually living.

"Finally, after searching for ten years, they found him here, in the West. This was the last place they looked for him because he had always hated America and things American. But they located him here and they organized to get him out of the way. It was about the same time that they found me and brought me into the work. I hardly liked an assassination scheme and told them so, but they swore that they would use me in some such way that I should not at least have to fire any bullet at a man whose back was turned to me.

"I joined in on that presumption. I entered the rodeo, and when Quinnado, or Alvarez as he calls himself, sent for me, I came. You know what followed. He called me by my real name, which is John Kobbe Turner. He made me the proposition you know of, and he bought me by letting me see your face.

"There is my whole story. And there's only one thing that I want to write at the end of it. Which is that I've succeeded in taking you away to freedom. And yet I've been half baffled, Miriam, by Quinnado, when I see what he has done. And when I saw how he has made himself respected and liked in this community, I began to doubt what my other friends had told me of him. I began to think that he *must* be an honest man, or if he was crooked before, he must have reformed."

"But you could not expect to know him as I know him," Miriam said. "He has never done anything except what he has figured out to be of benefit to himself. He has raised me for years, but it was because from the very first he had decided that someday he would marry me. And to effect that, he has kept me away from all young people, all . . ." Her voice broke with her anger. "Then we must go quickly, if we go at all."

He nodded. "I'll take you to the door of your room and wait for you there."

So they hurried out of the room and across the great hall where the moonlight had grown brighter, and up the steps and down the corridor to the door of her room. There they paused.

"Do you know," she whispered, "just now when I'm about to leave this house forever, I feel more deeply in his power than ever before? And just now I feel that he knows everything in my mind as clearly as if it were written out for him in black and white."

"Let him know what he pleases about you once we're outside this house."

"But how can we get through his guards?"

"They're posted to keep people out, not to keep them in."

She hesitated with her hand on the door. Then, with a lift of her head so that he almost saw her smiling up to him through the darkness, she opened the door quickly and stepped inside.

The door closed. He heard the faint falling of her steps as she crossed the room, and then—a sharp click and he knew that the door had been locked on the inside. Locked on the inside, and yet he had distinctly heard her walk away from it. Some other person was in that room.

XI

The first thought of Kobbe was that Alvarez had sent Jenkins or some other guard to the room of the girl to take charge of her and see that she did not escape from the house. This indicated that he had knowledge of the interview that had just passed between Kobbe and the girl. Miriam had been so confident that the rancher could not fail to read what was happening in her mind that she had almost persuaded Kobbe as well.

Yet he knew on second thought that there was no man he had seen on the place who would stand guard over the girl against her wish. Certainly Jenkins was not of that ilk.

There was a sound as if someone had stumbled and then recovered himself as softly as possibly. It came from the short flight of steps leading into the upper hall. Something else stirred at the opposite end of the hall, and the full meaning came to him instantly. They were blocking each end of the hall and were closing in on him. Alvarez had learned the purport of his talk with the girl and was more eager to destroy him than to use him for his own protection against his old enemies.

He looked eagerly and vainly around him for an escape, but the trap was nearly shut. There was only one possibility, and that was through the door into the room of the girl.

The stealthy sounds drew closer on either hand. When they came within arm's reach, he would die. He looked anxiously around him. Like all men in desperation, he began to feel about with his hands, as though the eyes were not enough. And, so doing, his fingertips touched the molding beside the door. The post was so massive that it thrust out a couple of inches from the main line of the wall. If it were so thick at the side, above the door lintel might be still deeper. He reached up and tested it. To his amazement he found that there was a ledge a full six inches deep.

After that he was in temporary safety for an instant, at the least. He caught hold on the ledge, swung himself sidewise and up like a pendulum, and managed to plant one foot on the ledge. Then he struggled up above the ledge. He would have fallen back, of course, from such a meager foothold, but he found that there were other projections to which he could cling, and he was able to turn around and finally to squat upon his heels and stare down into the darkness.

These stealthy sounds were gradually approaching down the hall on either side. But what was happening in the room of the girl? There was not a sound, not a whisper. And yet the walls were not at all soundproof. He had even been able to hear, from the hall, the light tapping of her feet as she had crossed the floor. And that was not all. He had heard the turning of the key within the lock. He knew that another person besides the girl was there, and yet not a whisper to tell him of what was happening came to his ears. It was a maddening suspense.

XII

What happened in the room of Miriam had been sufficiently horrible. She had crossed the room in the thick darkness and already had her hand upon the switch that would flood the room with electric light when she heard the click of the turning lock in the hall door. Yet it gave her only a momentary start. She attributed it, at once, to the touching of the outer knob of the door by Kobbe, who must be waiting there impatiently for her return. And when she returned to him, there would be an end to the long shadow of unhappiness in which she had lived. So she pulled the switch, and the lights poured through the room.

When she turned, she saw Alvarez with his back to the door and a smile on his pale face. It was the swift ending of her dream of success. She braced her hand against the table behind her and faced him with her teeth set.

He darkened, at that, and the smile faded from his face. It was the first time she had let him even have a hint of her true emotions concerning him. He recovered almost at once, however, and gestured toward the door to a little study that was part of her suite. There was nothing to do but to obey him. He could make her go by force, if he chose. And the silence of his movements, his use

254

of gestures in the place of words, showed that he knew that Kobbe was waiting for her outside the hall door. Waiting for her, at least, unless he had been alarmed by the noise of that turning lock. But in that case, what could he do?

She went into the study. Alvarez, still in silence, followed her and locked that door as well behind them.

"Now," he said, and his voice was as oily smooth as ever, "we can talk here quietly together. There are two doors and two walls between us and any disturbance."

"It is our last talk," she said, "and it will have to be a brief one."

He smiled, showing two perfectly even lines of white teeth, and for the first time she began to guess at what might happen, not to herself, but to Kobbe, who waited outside in the hall.

"I have been listening to you and my friend Kobbe," he said.

"Eavesdropping?" Miriam asked scornfully.

"An old habit of mine and a very useful one. A proud man does not do it. But I am not proud. If I had been proud, I should have died long ago."

"And now?" she asked.

"I am deciding at this moment what to do with him."

"With *Señor* Kobbe?"

"Use his right name!" snapped out Alvarez. "You know it as well as I do."

"Very good, *Señor* Quinnado."

He shrank as though she had struck him. And she instantly regretted that she had gone so far.

"I'm sorry," she said. "But . . . I want to know what you intend doing about him."

"About Kobbe . . . or Turner, to give him his right name? I have this moment made up my mind. He is to be removed, Miriam. He is to make an unfortunate attempt to escape. And he is to be unfortunately shot down by my overzealous guards. A regrettable affair, eh?"

Her lips stirred without making a sound.

"You are white, Miriam," he said. "This evidently cuts rather deeply."

"If you do that . . ."

"I am a devil, eh?"

"There is no word for you if you do that."

He had been walking slowly back and forth, but now he whirled around on her. "Miriam, you love him!"

"Love him? I have never seen him before today."

"I say that you love him."

"He is the finest man I have ever seen. He is the most honest and the most fearless. If I do not love him, at least, I honor him."

"And the word you have given me that we shall be married?"

"You dragged that promise out of me. Besides,

256

I promised to marry *Señor* Alvarez and not *Señor* Quinnado."

"That name again? And yet suppose, Miriam, that we make a bargain and that I marry you, after all?"

"I had rather die."

"Because you care so much for this Turner? This Kobbe?"

"Yes, yes. Because I care so much for him!"

"But he is mine, now."

"He will not be taken. There is something about him that cannot be beaten." Miriam's eyes shone.

"You will see. He is mine, Miriam. I'll offer you his life for the sake of your hand."

"You will marry me, knowing that I detest you?"

"Possession is the main thing. Everything else is an incident. You will understand better later on."

"What a hypocrite and liar you have been for these ten years."

"I have acted a part of the most consummate difficulty, and I have acted it better than it ever could have been acted upon the stage. That is the point of distinction. I am waiting for your answer, Miriam."

They were interrupted by a sound of scuffling and then voices loud enough to drift through the two walls to their ears from the inner hall of the house.

"Do you hear?" asked Alvarez. "They have taken him now, I believe."

He threw open the door. At once the noises were more audible. He ran across her bedroom and opened the door into the outer hall. Instantly a group of men struggled in, bringing Kobbe in their center. And there was a faint cry of grief and of terror from Miriam. Kobbe himself was furious rather than frightened. He was busy marking the faces of each of his captors. If he lived out the peril and met them again in freedom, it would go hard with all of them. That much was sure, and the grim expressions of his captors showed that they realized what they had done. He could hardly hope for mercy.

"We've got him, Alvarez," Jenkins announced. "And now that we have him, we're going to get rid of him, if you'll say the word. It can show up that we found him prowling around the house. They can never lay a hand on us for getting rid of him in that way. But if he's left alive, he's going to make these parts too hot to hold him and us, too. Understand?"

"Listen," pleaded Miriam at the shoulder of Alvarez. "Have him freed and I swear that I shall never see him again."

"And become the loving wife of Alvarez?"

She shuddered, but nodded.

"Very well, then, but it will require tact and patience. Let me talk with them first."

He turned toward the others and was about to speak when a window was thrown violently up from the side of the garden and a loud voice shouted into the room: "Quinnado!"

Alvarez whirled with a cry of terror so sharp that it was like the scream of a man in torture. The others saw only a pale blur and the glint of a gun in the darkness beyond the window. But what Alvarez saw made him scream: "Oñate!"

Then the gun spoke, and Quinnado pitched heavily upon his face.

That was the touch that freed the arms of Kobbe. He was instantly left to himself. Half of the men who had recently been busied in the care of him lunged for the garden window through which the avenger had fired. The other half stormed through the door and into the hall of the house. It left the two of them alone, and the instant they were free they fell into one another's arms.

But there was only an instant of that close embrace. The house was still filled with Alvarez's men, and what might happen when they returned from what would be doubtless a futile chase of the slayer could not be guessed.

Kobbe led Miriam swiftly from her room. They hurried down the hall, out through the flowers in the patio, and through the gate and on to the hilltop beyond. There was no time and no courage for them to go to the stables for a horse.

They had, above all, to make sure of their safety. El Capitán was left behind them, and they ran stumbling on through the night.

They ran blindly, as well, and yet it seemed to them both that they had found the very road of happiness.

Additional Copyright Information

About the Author

Max Brand is the best-known pen name of Frederick Faust, creator of Dr. Kildare, Destry, and many other fictional characters popular with readers and viewers worldwide. Faust wrote for a variety of audiences in many genres. His enormous output, totaling approximately thirty million words or the equivalent of five hundred thirty ordinary books, covered nearly every field: crime, fantasy, historical romance, espionage, Westerns, science fiction, adventure, animal stories, love, war, and fashionable society, big business and big medicine. Eighty motion pictures have been based on his work along with many radio and television programs. For good measure he also published four volumes of poetry. Perhaps no other author has reached more people in more different ways. Born in Seattle in 1892, orphaned early, Faust grew up in the rural San Joaquin Valley of California. At Berkeley he became a student rebel and one-man literary movement, contributing prodigiously to all campus publications. Denied a degree because of unconventional conduct, he embarked on a series of adventures culminating in New York City where, after a period of near starvation, he received simultaneous recognition as a serious poet and successful author of fiction. Later, he traveled widely, making his home in New York, then in Florence, and finally in Los Angeles. Once the United States entered the Second World War, Faust abandoned his lucrative writing career and his work as a screenwriter to serve as a war correspondent with the infantry in Italy, despite his fifty-one years and a bad heart. He was killed during a night attack on a hilltop village held by the German army. New books based on magazine serials or unpublished manuscripts or restored versions continue to appear so that, alive or dead, he has averaged a new book every four months for seventy-five years. Beyond this, some work by him is newly reprinted every week of every year in one or another format somewhere in the world. A great deal more about this author and his work can be found in *The Max Brand Companion* (Greenwood Press, 1997) edited by Jon Tuska and Vicki Piekarski. His website is www.MaxBrandOnline.com.

Books are produced in the United States using U.S.-based materials

Books are printed using a revolutionary new process called THINKtech™ that lowers energy usage by 70% and increases overall quality

Books are durable and flexible because of Smyth-sewing

Paper is sourced using environmentally responsible foresting methods and the paper is acid-free

Center Point Large Print
600 Brooks Road / PO Box 1
Thorndike, ME 04986-0001 USA

(207) 568-3717

US & Canada:
1 800 929-9108
www.centerpointlargeprint.com